EMMET D. WILLIAMS SCHOOL

PROJECT SOCIAL STUDIES

THIS DEAR-BOUGHT LAND

Harper & Row,

THIS
DEAR-BOUGHT
LAND

by Jean Lee Latham

PICTURES BY JACOB LANDAU

Publishers, New York and Evanston

THIS DEAR-BOUGHT LAND

Copyright © 1957 by Jean Lee Latham

Printed in the United States of America

Library of Congress catalog card number: 56–9439

CONTENTS

THIS DEAR-BOUGHT LAND

CHAPTER ONE

The Challenge

DAVID was dreaming he was aboard the *Golden Hind;*
Queen Elizabeth had just knighted Sir Francis Drake; in
another moment she would have knighted him, too; she
would have said, "Arise, Sir David Warren!"

But a rough hand shook him. Jem, the stableboy, said, "Master Davy!" And the dream was gone.

The good old days in England were gone; Drake was dead, the queen was dead, and James was king. And David Warren was no swashbuckling sea dog. He was fifteen and small for his age. "Takes after his mother's side," people always said. He could not remember his mother, but he knew he was not like his broad-shouldered, dark-bearded, bellowing father.

Jem shook him again. "You awake now, Master Davy? Sorry to bother you, but you said you wanted to go with me after holly. You awake?" His fingers bit into David's shoulder.

David clenched his teeth to keep from wincing. "Yes, I'm awake. I'll be at the stable in ten minutes."

"Aye, Master Davy." It was always the same; Jem's words respectful, his black eyes mocking. His voice saying, "Master Davy." His eyes saying, "I could break you in two with my bare hands!"

When Jem had clumped out and slammed the door, David threw back the covers, shivered in the raw December cold, and dashed to the fireplace. He was glad Jem had gone; Jem would have offered to warm his clothes for him. Not that I can blame him, David thought. I'm not much of a Warren.

Even Gran said that. "No sign of Warren in him." Sometimes she added, "Just as well! Heaven knows the Warren men haven't done anything sensible for the last four generations! *Sea dogs! Explorers!* Pah!"

Every time Gran fussed at Father, she went clear back

to Great-great-grandfather Warren, who had sailed with John Cabot. "Hare-brained fools!" she would say. But all the time her tongue was a wasp, her eyes were proud.

She would be scolding Father again today, about going to Virginia with the London Company. David sighed. If only he could be going with Father! What a dull place this would be without him. No one but Gran and Uncle Rupert and the servants. Nobody young but Jem. . . .

He jumped. How long had he been sitting here, with one boot on and the other in his hand? What if Jem had gone off without him? He finished dressing and hurried to the stable without stopping to eat.

Jem was still waiting. He smiled down at David. "You bundled up good and warm, Master Davy? I'll get the devil if I let you catch cold."

David clenched his teeth. If he yelled at Jem his voice might break and shoot up like a girl's. "I'm fine."

"Good, Master Davy! I'll lead the way and break trail, eh?" He tramped off through the snow, taking steps too long for David's stride to match. David floundered after him, soon out of breath.

Jem began to sing. David never got over the surprise of Jem's voice—high and clear and sweet.

> "Deck the hall with boughs of holly!
> Fa la la la la la la la la!
> 'Tis the season to be jolly!
> Fa la la la la la la la la!"

Jem looked back over his shoulder. "Why don't you sing, too, Master Davy?"

"I like to listen to you," David gasped.

3

Jem's laugh was a hoarse bark. The song began again, high and clear. He sang until they reached the woods.

All morning they gathered holly branches, stacking them into a mound that grew high as David's shoulder, then higher than his head.

"Not getting too tired, Master Davy?"

Hunger gnawed; his knees were shaking. David steadied his voice. "I'm all right."

Jem's black eyes mocked. "Good, Master Davy. Someone else will have to see about taking the holly home." He crouched by a hollow tree and pulled out a bundle wrapped in a piece of blanket. "This is good-by, Master Davy. Unless you'd like to walk to the village with me and see me off? If you're not too tired?"

Dumfounded, David stared at him. *Jem is running away! He knows I can't stop him!* For a moment it was so still he could hear the *drip-drip* of melting ice, and the soft *plop* as snow fell from the branches of trees. At last he said, "Yes, Jem, I'll walk to the village with you."

They slogged down the road through melting snow and mud. In the village they walked single file under the overhanging second stories of timbered houses to a sign that said The Three Bears.

Sailors crowded the long, low room of the tavern. A bearded man, sitting alone, looked up, grinned at Jem, then saw David. He scowled, heaved himself to his feet, and touched his forelock.

Jem said, "Bert, this is my friend, Davy. Tell him about our plan."

Bert waited until David was seated. Then he slumped

on the bench and growled, "I don't think the young gentleman will be interested in the likes of us."

"You're going to sea?" David asked. "Shipping out on an East Indiaman?"

"Nah!" Bert leaned his heavy forearms on the planked table. "No more of them East Indiamen for me! Mighty fine ships for the gentlemen that owns them. But what about the likes of us? Us that sails before the mast? Jammed in the fo'c'sle, living on weevily biscuit and stinking water—all for fourpence a day? No more of that!" He leaned forward, and his voice sank to a hoarse whisper. "We're going to Virginia! We'll sail before the mast, but when we get there, we'll jump ship and stay! A year —two years—in Virginia, and when we come back we'll be fine gentlemen, too!" He glared at David.

"I . . . see . . ." David said.

Bert stood, leaned forward, his hands flat on the table. "Do you now? You understand about the likes of us, eh? Us with no home, no land, no chance to better ourselves?" His words grated in his throat. "You that will always have houses and lands, no matter what you do? Hah! Come on, Jem!" He wheeled, straightened, and shoved through the crowd.

Jem got up. "Well, Davy, if anyone asks where I've gone, you can say you don't know, can't you?" His eyes mocked. "Of course, a Warren never lies, but you won't know where I am, will you? There's three ships sailing to Virginia. You won't know which one I'm on. You'll just know I'm *not* on the flagship, because that's where your father will be."

5

David swallowed hard. If only he could be going to Virginia, too! He forced himself to smile, and held out his hand. "Good luck, Jem."

The grip of Jem's calloused fingers made David wince in spite of himself. The black eyes mocked; this time his voice mocked, too. "That's my little man!" He swaggered away.

Dazed, his head spinning, David left the tavern and started down the muddy road. Bert never saw me before, he thought, but he hated me on sight. *You that will always have houses and lands, no matter what you do.*

The early winter dusk was closing in. David quickened his pace. An unarmed man was not safe on the roads after dark. Too many robber bands roving the countryside. He shivered, not from fear or the damp chill. Maybe, he thought, Jem hates me, too.

He reached their land, skirted the orchard and gardens, and entered the kitchen. Old Evans was turning a roast on a spit before the huge fireplace.

David sniffed and swallowed saliva. "I'd like a slice now, Evans."

"Aye, Master Davy." The old man stopped the spit, cut a slice, dripping juice, and laid it on a piece of bread. "At least you have an appetite like your father. Many's the time . . ." He stopped, cocked his head to listen, and smiled. Even in the kitchen, that far from the Great Hall, they could hear the rumble of Father's voice. Evans nodded. "They've been at it all day. Your father and your gran. Even that one has been chiming in." Evans always called Uncle Rupert *that one.* "How a fine lady like your mother had a brother like that one!"

6

"Is Uncle Rupert talking for Virginia, or against it?"

"Oh, that one is for it, of course! Hoping your father will die there, and he will get to run things until you're of a size to take over."

"But Gran is still talking against it?"

"Aye. Why she bothers, I'll never know. When Christopher Warren makes up his mind, the devil himself couldn't stop him." He chuckled, then sighed. "Be mighty different around here, when he's gone."

Suddenly David had had enough of his meat. He laid it down and went toward the sound of his father's voice.

As usual, Gran sat stiffly erect, stabbing at her needlework with angry jerks; Uncle Rupert slumped in his chair, his pale eyes staring over the peak of his matched fingertips; Father strode up and down, frowning one minute, laughing the next, bellowing.

He saw David, smiled, then turned back to his argument. "Mother, you know I can't stay here! Every ship that ever sailed for the glory of England has carried a Warren!"

Gran's needle stabbed; the thread rasped. "The more fools they," she said. "And you're the worst of the lot!"

Father grinned. "Started young enough, didn't I? Sailed before the mast with Drake. Clear around the world! No older than David when we started, but when we got back I was a man!"

"Didn't have any more sense than when you started," Gran said. "Off to Roanoke with that luckless crowd under Grenville. If Drake hadn't rescued the colony, you'd have died at Roanoke."

"We would not have died!" Father roared. "If we had hung on just two weeks longer—until our supply came—"

"Yes." Uncle Rupert sighed. "A pity. By now, England would have a profitable trade with the new world. Too bad you lost heart and gave up."

"I did not give up!" Father bellowed. "No Warren ever gives up! If I'd had my say, we'd have stayed!"

"And been lost like the second colony of Roanoke." Gran dropped her needlework, and leaned forward, gripping the arms of her chair. "Son, why can't you see this thing straight? America is not for the English! Why can't you see that? Why can't you Englishmen be satisfied? We have our homes, our fields, our gardens, our—"

"No, Mother." For once Father didn't bellow. "Not all Englishmen. We have outgrown our country. Five million people now. Our island has become a prison."

Uncle Rupert nodded. "Yes, if it hadn't been for the plague, the situation would be entirely out of hand. We really must do something with our excess population."

Gran snorted. "Then let the excess population go to America!"

"But, madam," Uncle Rupert explained, "you cannot depend on that sort to establish a profitable settlement. They'll do the work, of course. But there must be gentlemen there to plan and to rule."

Gran turned to Father again. "Christopher," she pleaded, "you're the last of my sons. That cursed land has taken the other three. Why must you die, too?"

Father shrugged. "Remember what Raleigh said? 'The wings of a man's life are plumed with the feathers of death.' We all have to die sometime, Mother."

8

"But why can't you be content to die comfortably at home?"

"Because I don't want to die comfortably!" Father bellowed. "I want to die fighting!"

"If you go to Virginia," Gran said, "you'll probably get your wish."

At the dinner table she picked up the argument again. "You don't think Spain is going to stand by and do nothing while we try to colonize Virginia, do you? If you meet a Spanish man-of-war, she'll sink all three of your ships. Or if you get as far as the West Indies, you may die there. Killed by a poisoned arrow."

Father grinned. "Oh, no! The natives are cannibals. No poisoned arrows. Wouldn't want to spoil their food."

Uncle Rupert choked and gagged.

Father laughed, wiped his mouth, and got up. "How about it, David? Can you be ready to start for London in half an hour?"

"S-s-s-sir? I mean, yes, sir!"

"Pack you a change of shirts, and you may stay with me till the ships weigh anchor."

Gran stared. "You didn't tell me you're leaving tonight! Before Christmas!"

Father chuckled. "By Christmas, we'll be on the high seas, a third of the way to Virginia! Hurry along, David."

"Yes, sir!" David was halfway up the stairs when he heard Gran speak again.

"Christopher! You're not planning to take that boy with you?"

David stopped, his heart hammering. Maybe he was going to go to Virginia!

9

Father's laughter rumbled. "Take David? Hardly! Give him another five years, and he may pass for a Warren. But not now."

No . . . not now. David sighed and went for his change of shirts.

When he came down Old Evans waited with three horses—two saddled, and one loaded with Father's luggage. They plodded down the road, single file, first Father, then David, leading the pack horse behind him. His last trip with Father for no one knew how long. Why couldn't he think of something to say? The minutes dragged.

"You'll like Captain Newport," Father said. "Another of Drake's sea dogs."

"Yes, sir." Another long silence.

"Sorry to be leaving you with no man but Rupert to talk to, David. But you understand how it is?"

"Yes, sir."

"This time we cannot fail! Spain has Florida; the French are settling the north. It's our last chance, David. If England fails again—"

They had not heard a sound until men sprang at them from both sides, seizing their horses' heads, swinging heavy clubs.

When David opened his eyes, he lay in the muddy road. The horses were gone. A before-dawn gray silvered the trees. His father's body made a dark sprawl on a patch of snow.

"Father!" He tried to stand, staggered, and crawled to kneel beside him.

His father was still breathing, but in great, tearing

gasps, as though hungry for air. His eyes stared blankly a moment, then focused. "Tell—Newport—you—in my place."

"Yes, Father!"

"On every ship . . ." He sighed, his eyes closed, his jaw went slack.

Stumbling and falling, picking himself up and stumbling again, David ran to the house.

Old Evans was in the kitchen. "Master Davy!"

Only then did David begin to shake. His teeth chattered as he told Evans. "You'll have to take care of—things," he finished. "I must get to London before Captain Newport sails. A—a—message from Father."

"Aye, lad. You'll have to go. You're the only Warren left."

Captain Newport was at Blackwall, in his cabin aboard the *Susan Constant*, talking to a pudgy, gray-bearded man. The captain's smile was warm. "Christopher Warren's son, eh?" He nodded toward the pudgy man. "This is Mr. Wingfield, David. Another friend of your father's."

Mr. Wingfield shook hands. His voice was high and thin. "You've come to see your father off?"

David swallowed and looked at Captain Newport. It would be easier to tell him, he thought, if he didn't make me think so much of Father. He hoped he could say what he had to say without his chin shaking or his voice shooting up.

When David had finished, Captain Newport stared at him, wordless.

Mr. Wingfield sighed. "A dastardly business. I hope the day will come soon when we can ship those scoundrels off to America and put them to useful work. Dastardly!" He patted David's shoulder. "Of course you shall go with us, David. Your father invested heavily in the London Company. It's only right that his son should share in the glory. Eh, Newport?"

Captain Newport did not answer. He ran his hand through his dark hair. His eyes were troubled. When the door opened, he jumped up, as though glad of the interruption. "Ah, Captain Smith! Come in, man! Come in!"

Captain Smith was shorter than Newport, with a well-muscled, sturdy look, and impatient frown lines between stern blue eyes. His tanned face was almost as brown as his beard. David's heart sank. They all looked so old and stern. How could he take his father's place among them?

When Newport introduced David, Captain Smith smiled, and seemed to lose ten years. Relief eased the tightness in David's chest. Captain Smith's not so old, he thought. I'm glad there's somebody younger.

Mr. Wingfield told what had happened. "So, of course," he said, "we shall take David with us."

"*What!*" The frown lines deepened between John Smith's eyes. His glance whipped over David's scrawny body, his white hands. "Wingfield, have some sense! This venture is no place for women and children!"

David felt his face get hot. "I'm no child, sir! I'm fifteen!"

Captain Smith hooked his thumbs in his belt. "My little tuffety-taffety gentleman, we are carrying a quarter of a ton of supplies for every man on this expedition! Just what would you do in Virginia to make you worth your keep?"

"He shall go as my footman!" Wingfield said. "I'll be personally responsible for him!"

John Smith snorted, turned his back on Wingfield, and looked at Newport.

Captain Newport's eyes were still troubled. "Christopher Warren always said, 'Every ship that ever sailed for the glory of England has carried a Warren.'"

David nodded. "Yes, sir! Just—just—the other night—" His voice shook. He clenched his teeth, then went on. "Just the other night, he said, 'I sailed before the mast with Drake. No older than David when we started, but when we got back, I was a man!'"

John Smith cocked his head. "Now, there's an idea, Captain Newport! Let him sail before the mast." His smiling eyes challenged David. "Think you could live in the fo'c'sle, and work as a common sailor? Think you're as much of a man as your father was?"

David glared into the bronzed face. Some day, he thought, some day, Captain John Smith, you'll eat those words! Still glaring at John Smith, he said, "Captain Newport, sir, I'd consider it an honor to sail before the mast with you!"

The crow's-feet deepened around Smith's eyes. His bearded lips twitched. "There you are, Captain Newport! Everything taken care of!" He swaggered out of the cabin.

13

CHAPTER TWO

Before the Mast

MR. WINGFIELD glared after John Smith. "That up-start! Why in the name of heaven the London Company—"

Captain Newport frowned. "He's a capable man, Wing-field. Not many men can fight a battle, navigate a ship, and chart a map."

"But he's no gentleman born!"

"In Virginia," Newport said, "we may have more need of capable men than of gentlemen born. Ever thought of that?"

Wingfield did not answer. He laid his pudgy hand on David's shoulder. "Forget about sailing before the mast, David. Just because that bragging upstart challenged you—"

"I want to sail before the mast!" David declared. "I'll make that man eat his words!"

Captain Newport nodded. "Very well, David. We'll sign you on."

"Newport, no!" Wingfield's voice sharpened. "I absolutely forbid it!"

"Mr. Wingfield!" Captain Newport laid his hand on a small box, closed and sealed. "The names of the Council for Virginia are in this box. I presume your name is on the list. But, until we get to Virginia, and I break the seals and open the box—I am in charge."

"Yes, yes, of course, but—"

"In absolute charge! My word is law!" He sent for his first mate. "Mr. Hodges, here is a new hand for the fo'c'sle."

Mr. Hodges opened his mouth and shut it again. At last he said, "Aye, aye, sir. What name, sir?"

"David Warren!" Mr. Wingfield shrilled. "Christopher Warren's son! His father was killed, and David is going to Virginia in his stead. And if I—" He faced Captain Newport's level stare, and stopped.

Mr. Hodges looked at his captain. "We've a pretty hard lot in the fo'c'sle, sir. The lad will get along better if they don't know he's a gentleman."

Newport nodded. "Put him down as Davy . . . Beach. And about clothes . . . Think you've slops small enough for him?"

Mr. Hodges walked around David, studying him, shaking his head.

"Send Tim with the smallest you have." Newport ordered.

Mr. Hodges eyed David once more and departed. In a few moments a lively old man, with a leather-brown face and bright little eyes, came to the cabin.

He grinned and pulled his forelock. "Slops for the younker, sir."

"Strip, David," Newport ordered.

David didn't mind shedding his velvet and ruffles for the coarse shirt and jacket, the trousers and sash. What made his ears burn was Tim's eyes taking his measure.

Newport said, "I'm turning him over to you to train, Tim."

"Aye, aye, sir!" The old man said nothing more until they had left the cabin. Outside, though, he clutched David's arm. "Davy, lad, listen! I don't know what you're running *from!* But it ain't as bad as what you're running *to!* Jump ship while you have a chance! The fo'c'sle's no place for you! You wouldn't last—"

"I've signed on for Virginia," David said. "And you are to train me. Captain's orders. If you don't obey captain's orders, that's mutiny!"

Tim sighed and shrugged. "You'll get enough of it before we sail." He led the way forward.

A huge, red-bearded man blocked their path, and stared with little pig eyes buried in fat. "So that's our new hand?"

"Don't worry, Red; I'll learn him," Tim promised.

"I'll learn him, too." The pig eyes glittered; the loose grin threatened.

Behind David a voice snapped, "Red Wally! The lad is smart as paint! Before we get to Virginia, I expect him to be able to hand, reef, and steer!"

David turned. Captain Smith stood there, the frown lines deep between his eyes, glaring up at the huge fellow, who towered head and shoulders above him.

Red's bluster died. He touched his forelock. "Aye, aye, sir! Any friend of yours is bound to be smart! We'll take good care of the younker, sir!" He ambled off.

David flared. "I don't need any help from—"

"Don't speak till you're spoken to! And when you do, say *sir!*" The captain wheeled and strode aft.

"You're lucky he's a friend of yours," Tim said.

David spoke through his teeth. "He's no friend of mine, and I'm no friend of his! And some day—"

Tim patted his shoulder. "Then let's keep it a secret between us, Davy. Red's as mean as a Muscovy wolf, but he fought with the captain once. If he thinks you're a friend—"

"I'm not going to—"

Tim's voice was mild. "Stow your gab and keep it stowed. I'm to learn you, not to listen to you. Now, what do you know?"

"Why—why—in Latin I was reading—"

"And stow that, too. Do you know bow from stern? Starboard from larboard? Can you box a compass, or heave a lead? Can you figure your speed?"

"No, sir. I don't know anything, sir."

"Then that's where we begin. Maybe you'll have time to learn something before we sail. Figure I might as well make you clever with your hands. You won't throw much weight on a halyard. Don't want to send you aloft too soon. Someone might shake you off, just for fun. Be all right if you hit the water, but you might hit the deck. We'll start with knots."

All morning David worked with the stiff, tarry line until his hands were blistered; he worked until the blisters broke and bled. He tried to cast a hand lead, caught his ankle in a coil, and was jerked, yelling, over the side into the icy water. He came up, gasping and choking.

A huge hand grabbed him and secured a line around him. Red bellowed, "Heave away!"

They pulled David up, and Red followed, climbing hand over hand up a single line.

"Th-thank you," David gasped.

Red cursed him roundly, then growled, "Don't thank me! Thank the captain! If I'd let you drown, he'd run me through and roast me for breakfast! Go down to the galley and help the cook till you dry out."

Food! Maybe the cook would give him a slice of roast beef or . . . In the galley, he saw the cook stirring a huge pot of grayish slime, with pieces of salt pork floating on top.

The cook lifted a ladleful of the soup. "You hungry, lad?"

David gagged. "No, sir, not a bit!"

"Hope you get your sea legs soon, so you can eat while the grub is still good." He opened another huge pot and David smelled meat browning.

"What's that?"

"For the gentlemen's mess." He stirred the grayish slime again. "You're sure you're not hungry?"

"No, sir!" All I want, he thought, is to get in my bed and . . . "Where do we sleep?" he asked.

"You? In the fo'c'sle."

"I didn't see any beds."

"Beds? You sleep on the floor." He turned to eye David up and down. "Just what are you doing in the fo'c'sle?"

David stiffened. "I signed on for Virginia!"

"Hmmm. . . . Well, it'll be a few days yet before we sail."

For a week, while they were still at anchor, David worked with knots and lines. He climbed, shivering, up the foremast, carrying a bucket of rancid grease. Gagging, he scooped it up with his hand and slathered it on the mast.

Below, gentlemen in velvet and lace came and went, laughed, and threw coins to three musicians who played for them. How much longer? When would they sail? How soon would they get to Virginia?

Friday, the nineteenth of December, the sailors stowed the last of the cargo, covered the hatches with tarpaulins and battened them down. They closed all the ports and wedged them shut. The air between decks grew foul. David, on an errand below, was glad to come topside again.

"Don't they have any air to breathe till we get to Virginia?" he asked Tim.

"After we're under way, lad, the wind sails carry the air below." He showed David a canvas tube, with a wide, funnel-shaped mouth, held open by a hoop. "That runs down through the hatches to the holds. When we're moving, the wind blows into this funnel and down through the wind sail and out the bottom. So it's not so bad then. Of course, it's not so good, either."

"We're better off in the fo'c'sle, aren't we?"

"Some ways. Some ways we're not. Come a heavy sea over the bow, and we catch it. And when the ship pounds, we catch it, too."

At two bells of the afternoon watch, the ship was snug. The masters of the other two ships came aboard the *Susan Constant*, and stood on the poop, studying the sky, talking with Newport. Captain Gosnold, commanding the *Godspeed*, was fair, with quiet gray eyes and a solid look. Captain Ratcliffe, commanding the *Discovery,* the little twenty-ton pinnace, was a tall, ruddy-faced man, with narrow, heavy-lidded eyes that did not seem to go with his easy smile.

"Don't know about Captain Ratcliffe," old Tim said, "but the other two are master mariners. Gosnold's been to America before. To somewhere called 'Cape Cod.' Named an island for his little girl. Called it 'Martha's Vineyard.' And Newport—he sailed with Drake!"

My father sailed with Drake! The words were on David's tongue, but he had learned to keep his tongue between his teeth. He wasn't a Warren here; he was Davy Beach. Tolerated in the fo'c'sle because Red thought he was a friend of John Smith's.

On the poop, the conference of the masters ended. Newport's bellow reached the fo'c'sle. "Blast the barometer! We sail with the tide in the morning!"

Red grinned. "Aye, and he'll crowd sail!"

Old Tim beckoned Davy outside. "Look, lad, it's your last chance. After we've sailed, and you find you can't—"

"I signed on for Virginia!"

Tim sighed and left him. Late that afternoon, when David was wrapping a tarry line with chafing gear, he looked up to find Captain Smith standing over him.

"Well, David?"

David straightened, and touched his forelock. "Am I to speak, sir?"

"You've been spoken to!" The captain took hold of David's wrist and studied his hand—blackened with tar, the cracks and blisters half healed and raw again. "Had about enough of the fo'c'sle?"

David met the captain's gaze squarely. "I signed on for Virginia, sir."

John Smith's eyes twinkled. "Don't like me much, do you?" He slapped David's shoulder. "That's all right! You have lots of company!" And, chuckling as though pleased with himself, he swaggered aft.

Morning dawned with skies heavily overcast. David saw Captain Ratcliffe pacing the deck of the little *Discovery*, scanning the heavens.

Captain Newport came topside, cast a casual glance up, and said, "All right, Mr. Hodges."

Mr. Hodges eyed the scudding clouds. "Aye, aye, sir."

The *Susan Constant* weighed anchor first, then the *Godspeed*, then the *Discovery*. Soon the little pinnace was wallowing and falling behind.

Mr. Hodges watched her. "We'll have to reef sail or we'll lose her, sir."

Newport shrugged. "She'll have to carry sail."

"She's heavy-laden, sir. She's wallowing, scuppers under."

"Her timbers can take it."

Red grinned. "Drake's man, all right!"

They sailed east, down the Thames. The wind rose in sharp, spiteful gusts, then veered, and caught them on the port beam. They fought to escape being driven aground, and were forced to anchor. The *Susan Constant* pitched and rolled.

All over the ship David heard men retching and vomiting. I'm glad I haven't been eating, he thought. I haven't had enough food to . . .

But he found that not eating did not secure him against seasickness. In the fo'c'sle they jeered at him. Red thrust food in his face—gobs of pork, dripping grease, hunks of salt beef.

"Don't worry! You'll learn to eat it!" Red promised. "You'll learn to eat anything that holds still!"

David fled to the rail again. *How much longer?* Father had said that by Christmas they would be on the open sea, well on their way to Virginia. Here it was, the twenty-second, and they were still in the Thames. How much longer? Would he be sick all the way to America?

Christmas Eve, they were still wind-bound in the Thames, but David had found his sea legs. When the cook asked for his help, he swaggered to the galley.

"Hungry, lad?" the cook asked.

"Yes!" David declared. "And I can eat anything that holds still!"

The cook was roasting a pig for the gentlemen aft.

Even the fo'c'sle would have baked hash, and steamed pudding with raisins.

From some hiding place the crews brought out holly and evergreens to decorate the ships. That night battle lanterns flared in the riggings and fiddlers played. The men on the *Discovery* began to sing "God Rest You Merry, Gentlemen." David heard Jem's voice rise, high and clear. The others stopped singing, and Jem finished the song alone.

Captain Newport lifted his trumpet and hailed the pinnace. "Have that man sing again!"

Jem's voice, with a more piercing sweetness than David had ever heard before, began "The Coventry Carol."

"Lul-lay, Thou little tiny Child . . ."

Blindly, David turned and edged his way aft to a place of hiding in the shadow of the high poop. He crouched there, shuddering. All the Christmas Eves he had ever known, all his memories of his father, tore at his throat. He heard footsteps, and fought to stifle his sobs. He bit his hand until he tasted blood.

Someone was standing near him by the rail. David stared up through his tears. The flicker of a lantern touched Captain Smith's face. David was glad he was hidden in the shadows.

The song was ending. The last note swelled, then faded and faded until David did not know whether he was still hearing the sound or only remembering it. He heard a sniff, and looked up again. John Smith had turned, and was staring out across the water. Was he homesick, too?

Was he remembering other Christmas Eves? David started to rise.

"Captain Smith!" someone yelled. "Can you lead us in 'Wassail'?"

Smith wheeled, hooked his thumbs in his belt, lifted his chin, and bellowed, "I can lead you in anything! I can lead you anywhere! But can you follow?" He swaggered forward to a welcoming roar of laughter. In a moment his voice was biting out the words, with a punching, insistent rhythm that started the men on all three ships stamping and shouting:

> "Wassail, wassail, all over the town!
> Our bread it is white and our ale it is brown!"

A good thing, David thought, that I didn't let him catch me bawling!

The next day the wind was fair, and they reached the mouth of the Thames.

"Hurrah for the open sea!" Red shouted.

"Might help," Tim said, "and again it mightn't."

Red grabbed a handful of Tim's shirt. "Stow your bad-luck talk and keep it stowed! Or I'll ram it down your throat! When we've got sea room . . ."

But having sea room did not help. A full gale struck them, and for days they tacked against it, trying to make headway. A week passed. They were still north of the Straits of Dover, in sight of the eastern coast of England. When would they ever get through the English Channel, into the Atlantic, and be on their way?

After three weeks, Captain Newport gave up the struggle to tack against the gales. The ships came to anchor, almost in sight of the Thames. All day and all night the *Susan Constant* rolled and pitched and fought her cable. Another week passed.

The drinking water began to stink. In the fo'c'sle the men snapped and snarled. Aft, the gentlemen gathered in knots and argued. They seemed to be quarreling about everything, too. Time and again David heard John Smith's voice shouting down the others.

"Bah! No need to drown if you keep your head about you! I remember when I was thrown overboard off the Isle of St. Mary . . ."

"Nonsense! That ship was iron sick! Every bolt in her rusted through! If we'd taken her . . ."

A bragging upstart, Mr. Wingfield had said. *A capable man,* Captain Newport had called him. What was John Smith, anyhow?

Twice David heard him get into an argument with Mr. Wingfield.

"Hah! I made a better bomb than that! I remember when I helped lift the siege of Alba Regalis. I told the Earl of Meldritch . . ."

"Nonsense! If you have your wits about you, you can defeat an army twice your number, any day! I remember once when we faced twenty thousand Turks . . ."

Red, who was listening, grinned at David, and nodded. "I was with him that time! Never saw a man like the captain! Not another man living can think as fast when death is breathing down his neck!"

Not many men, Newport had said, *can fight a battle, navigate a ship, and chart a map.*

Another week dragged by. More quarrels smoldered and flared. After six long weeks—they should have been near America by now—the winds at last favored them, and they cleared the English Channel, reached the Atlantic, and turned south on the long voyage to Virginia.

For a few days the men were cheerful; then quarrels began again. Aft, the gentlemen did not shout so much, but they gathered in groups and muttered.

For three days something nagged at David's mind; what was wrong? Then he realized what was puzzling him; he had not heard the captain shouting. Something must be wrong. He asked old Tim if he had heard anything about the captain.

Tim shook his head, then grinned. "You're just like Red. When you say 'the captain' you mean John Smith. Decided he's a friend of yours?"

David flushed, then grinned, too. "I've decided one thing: he's a capable man, just like Newport said. We'll need him in Virginia."

Off the Canaries, Captain Newport signaled his captains. They came aboard the flagship and joined him on the poop. Drums rolled; a hoarse voice bawled, "All hands on deck!"

What now?

Captain Newport said, "Bring the prisoner!"

Two soldiers shoved someone toward the poop. David heard Red gasp, then begin to curse. The prisoner was John Smith.

CHAPTER THREE

"Stand by for Sounding!"

"JOHN SMITH," Captain Newport said, "you are accused of plotting mutiny."

Captain Smith's head jerked up; he started to speak.

But Newport motioned for silence. "When you stand trial, you will have a chance to answer the charges against you. For the rest of the journey, you will be a prisoner aboard the *Discovery*."

The accused man stood motionless. Then, without a word, he unbuckled his sword and presented it to Captain Newport. Looking neither right nor left, he saluted, turned, and went over the side with his guards. Captain Newport wheeled and went below. A babble of astonishment ran over the deck of the flagship.

Numb with bewilderment, David stood by old Tim and watched as John Smith went aboard the *Discovery*, and disappeared down a companionway. Behind David, someone gave a little grunt of satisfaction. He turned. Mr. Wingfield stood there, eying the pinnace.

Tim touched his forelock. "What will happen to him, sir?"

Mr. Wingfield smiled grimly. "He'll be sent back to London, to stand trial for mutiny! That's what will happen!" He patted David's shoulder. "Well, David Warren, no reason now to stay in the fo'c'sle, eh? Just because that scoundrel challenged you? High time you came aft, where you belong, among the gentlemen!"

David felt his ears get hot. *He's not a scoundrel! He's twice the man you are!* He wanted to shout the words, but he only said, "Is it captain's orders, sir? That I come aft?"

Mr. Wingfield flushed. "What do you mean?"

"Unless it's captain's orders, sir, I'd rather stay in the fo'c'sle."

"Why—you—you—" Mr. Wingfield spluttered. He strode away, still fuming.

"So that's who you are," Tim said. "Christopher Warren's son."

David nodded.

"And you could go aft, among the gentlemen? Then why in the name of sense don't you go?"

David looked down at his dirty, scarred hands. He remembered John Smith's smiling eyes. *Think you're as much of a man as your father was?* He grinned, shrugged, and did not answer.

Tim clutched his arm. "Davy, lad, go! When scurvy hits, the men in the fo'c'sle die first!"

"Scurvy?"

"It's a sickness—because of the food, they say. When men are too long at sea. And we're going to be too long at sea on this voyage, lad. We should have been nigh to Virginia before we cleared the English Channel!"

David straightened. "My father sailed before the mast with Drake. Clear around the world. I guess I'll last till Virginia."

A week later, the first man died of scurvy.

"Davy, lad . . ." Tim said.

David shook his head.

Four times in the week that followed, Master Hunt, their minister, read the burial service. A body, wrapped in its sheet, weighted with cannon shot, slid into the water.

Captain Ratcliffe signaled from the *Discovery*, and a boat put out, carrying Master Hunt to the pinnace, to read the burial service there. David's heart hammered, his tongue was stiff in his mouth, as he waited for Master Hunt to return.

"Was it Captain Smith, sir?"

"No, David. One of the men from the fo'c'sle."

Ten times, first on one ship, then another, Master Hunt read the service, and a sheeted body slid into the water.

"Davy, lad . . ." Tim said again.

David did not answer. He only asked, "A prisoner—do they take good care of him? Feed him all right?"

They reached the West Indies, lowered the sick men into boats, and carried them ashore to lie on the sand. Natives came in canoes, bringing fresh fruit—pineapples and bananas. The men who were on their feet fed the sick men first.

David had watch duty aboard the *Susan Constant*. He climbed aloft, where he could keep an eye on the *Discovery*. He saw men carry Jem's friend, Bert, ashore. He saw Jem, brown and brawny, beaching a boat with one heave of his mighty shoulders. No sign of John Smith. Weren't they going to let him go ashore? Or were they going to keep him in the smothering heat between decks?

When his watch ended, David went ashore, took five steps, and stopped, bewildered. The ground was moving beneath his feet!

Jem, who was passing, looked back over his shoulder to laugh. "It's solid ground, all right, mate! You don't have your land legs yet!"

Mate. Jem didn't recognize him! David called, "Thank you, Jem!"

Jem wheeled. "Master Davy! What—where—" Even after David had explained what happened, Jem stared, agape.

David picked up a pineapple, slashed it twice, thrust his face in a quarter, gnawing and sucking the juice.

"You in the fo'c'sle!" Jem said. For once his eyes did not mock. Twice he opened his mouth to say something else, and stopped. "Well, I've got to help take care of our sick." He started away.

"How's the—the prisoner?" David asked.

Jem shrugged. "I don't know. We never see him. He's somewhere between decks."

Alone, David finished the pineapple, and reached for another. *Somewhere between decks. . . .* Suddenly he picked up an armload of fruit and went to one of the boats from the *Discovery*. Could he make the sailor believe him?

He spoke loudly, in an offhand fashion. "I'm to feed the prisoner. Captain Newport's orders."

The sailor glowered at him, then spoke through his teeth. "They want to keep him alive till they hang him, eh?"

David's stomach lurched. "Hang him?"

"What do you think they do with mutineers?" He rowed David to the pinnace.

The watch on board challenged him and stared at him suspiciously. David's manner was even more offhand. "I'm to feed the prisoner. Captain Newport's orders!"

The sailor muttered something, nodded, and directed David with a jerk of his thumb. David went below, into the stifling heat. Poor fellow, he thought. Disgraced, his spirit broken, huddled down here in chains! I'm going to tell him . . . He found John Smith, and stared, bewildered.

The captain had a board across two kegs for a table, and was busy writing. He did not look up.

David was glad he had practiced his speech. "I'm to feed the prisoner. Captain Newport's orders, sir."

John Smith finished a page, laid it aside, and cocked an eyebrow. "Did you get aboard with that lie?"

"What? I mean, what, sir?" Silence. David grinned feebly. "Aye, aye, sir. I told it twice."

"When you get back ashore, go to Captain Ratcliffe and confess—if you're man enough."

David's ears burned. He slammed the fruit down on a keg. "You think I'm afraid to?"

"I'm thinking of the poor fools you tricked into letting you come aboard. They're the ones who will suffer for it. Now get out."

David's ears were still burning when he hunted up Captain Ratcliffe. Standing stiff as a poker, he confessed. "And, if you please, sir, I wish you'd punish me instead of the two men I lied to."

"Hmmm. . . ." The hooded eyes studied him. "Ever had a taste of the cat-o'-nine-tails?"

David had seen a man spread-eagled on a grating, while the leather thongs cut red gashes in his back. His heart hammered until he could hear it beating in his ears. "No, sir."

"But you want to stand punishment for all three?"

David wet his lips. "Yes, sir."

Ratcliffe smiled his easy smile, and clapped David on the shoulder. "Spoken like a man! For the rest of the time ashore, you shall have charge of feeding the prisoner. And I'll forget about punishing the other two. How's that?"

"Thank, you, sir!"

"Did you take him fresh water?"

"No, sir."

"Then do it." He clapped David on the shoulder again. "Tell him you're not lying this time; it's Captain Ratcliffe's orders."

"Thank you, sir!" Back on the *Discovery* again, David

33

faced John Smith and explained about his "punishment."
Silence. "I—I—think Captain Ratcliffe was very kind to
—I mean—not to—"

"Captain Ratcliffe," John Smith barked, "took a coward's way out."

"Sir?"

"If he doesn't punish you, he doesn't have to admit
that his watch is not dependable."

"Oh. . . ."

"Well, if you're going to be in and out of here, you
might as well learn something. I'm writing a book for
young seamen."

"A *book* for sailors? I'd think—"

"That all he needs is brawn and skill? If he ever expects to command a ship, he needs some brains, too. Here
—see if you have any brains." He handed David a few
pages and turned back to his writing.

I'll show him! David told himself. I'll show him! And
he began to read, making a fierce attempt to remember
every word.

After a while, the captain looked up. "Well, have you
learned anything?"

"Yes, sir! I know why the binnacle is nailed together
with wooden pins, instead of with iron. If you got iron
that close to the compass, it would pull the needle away
from the north."

"That all?"

David grinned. This was really going to surprise the
captain. "And I can figure how tall the mainmast is on
the *Golden Hind*."

John Smith's eyes did open at that. "So?"

"Yes, sir. Her breadth is eighteen feet, and her main-mast is four-fifths as high as the ship is wide, so—" He stopped when the captain snorted. "But it says so! Right here!" He read:

Masts are proportioned to the beam. If a ship be overmasted, either in length or thickness—a taunt mast—she will labor too much. The rule most used for the length of the mainmast is four-fifths of a yard of length for every foot of beam, and an inch of thickness for every yard—

He stopped reading. "Oh . . . yards. Then the main-mast on the *Golden Hind* is fifteen *yards.*"

"And not fifteen *feet!*" the captain growled. Suddenly he smiled. "But you do have a way with figures. Get over your carelessness, and I'll teach you to survey and to chart a map." He started writing again.

"You—you—must be a lot older than you look. I mean —to know so many things."

John Smith's eyes twinkled. "I'm twenty-eight. But I've fought to learn just as hard as I've fought to win a battle."

"Why?"

The frown lines came back. "Because I was born igno-rant! Just as you were! And the only way to overcome ignorance is by fighting to learn! *Fighting!*"

"Don't you ever stop fighting?"

"No! *To overcome is to live!*" Still frowning, he bent over his work again. "You'd better go ashore now. Always learn everything you can, anywhere you are. You never know when it will come in handy."

"Aye, aye, sir!" David straightened and made a snappy salute. The captain did not look up, but David was still smiling when he reached the shore.

For three weeks he divided his time between learning about the islands where they stopped and studying with John Smith. The second week in April, when the sick men had recovered, Captain Newport gave the order to wood and water the ships for the final part of their voyage. A cheer went up.

David yelled, too, then stopped. When he returned to the *Susan Constant* . . .

The evening before they were to sail he went aboard the *Discovery* for the last time with food for the prisoner. John Smith smiled at him.

David grinned back. "I wonder, sir," he suggested, "if they don't need another hand on the *Discovery?*"

"You?"

"Aye, aye, sir."

John Smith glared. "No! You will go back to your post on the flagship! And if you have a grain of sense, you will never mention my name!"

"But I don't believe you plotted mutiny! I—"

"What you believe or don't believe won't save my neck." He slammed his hand flat on the table. "This is no game for children! Go back to your ship, and keep your tongue between your teeth! That's an order! Now get out and stay out!"

Seething, David returned to the flagship. Some day, he thought, when I'm big enough, I'll fight that man with my bare fists!

The next morning they got under way. When they catted the huge, dripping anchor, Red grinned. "We won't wet that again till we're in Virginia! Fair sailing now! Our troubles are over!"

"Maybe," Tim said, "and maybe not."

Red laughed and winked at David. "Tim always was the gloomy one! Never a cheerful word!"

At noon the fourth day out from the West Indies, Captain Newport shot the sun and passed the word. "We've crossed the Tropic of Cancer. In four days, we'll sight Virginia. A week from now, we'll be settled!"

Red slapped Tim on the back. "Virginia in four days!"

"Maybe," Tim said, "and maybe not. I'm never sure of a landfall till I see the loom of the land."

Red winked at David again.

Four days passed. Five. No sight of land. From dawn until darkness closed down the lookouts perched high, searching the emptiness. The sixth day dawned; still no land.

Captain Ratcliffe signaled and asked for a conference. He and Captain Gosnold came aboard the flagship and went below to Newport's cabin. On deck, men listened, tense and silent.

Presently Ratcliffe's voice rose in anger. "The truth of it is—we're lost! I say we'd better go back while we've got supplies to get back!" The voices died to a mutter; Ratcliffe shouted again. "Sir, I'm in command of the *Discovery!* I'm responsible for the lives of my passengers! I'm—"

Newport's bellow swept the ship. "You're under my

37

command! I'll give orders and you'll obey! Our course is west! Due west!"

The captains came topside. Ratcliffe and Gosnold returned to their ships. Newport spoke to his first mate, and his words rang over the ship again. "Due west, Mr. Hodges, and hold your course!"

That night David slept uneasily and wakened to shouts. "All hands on deck!" He jumped to his feet, sprawled, scrambled up again, and lurched from the fo'c'sle. A *boom* like a cannon's roar told him a sail had burst. Rain poured, the wind howled, and the *Susan Constant*, stripped of every sail, scudded under bare poles for the open sea.

He had thought he was seasoned to a sailor's life, but for three days and nights he lived in terror. Near two bells of the forenoon watch the fourth morning the storm ended, though great waves still pounded the ship. At morning service, Master Hunt read the Prayer of Thanksgiving:

"The waters of the sea well nigh covered us; the proud waters had well nigh gone over our souls. The sea roared and the stormy wind lifted the waves thereof. We were carried up as it were to heaven and then down again unto the deep. . . ."

The words did not comfort David. The *Susan* had survived, but what of the others? What of the *Godspeed*? What of the little *Discovery*?

Captain Newport lifted his trumpet. "Fire a signal."

A cannon *boomed*. They held their breath to listen. No answer.

Time and again, all morning and well into the afternoon, they fired the cannon and listened. At last, so faintly that David wondered if he imagined it, a faint *boom* answered from the north, and another from the east. To-ward sunset the three ships were together again. None had sighted land.

"Stand by for sounding!" Newport ordered. The deep-sea lead found no bottom. The captain's face was rock hard.

Ratcliffe's voice came over the restless, empty ocean. "Where are we now?"

"East of Virginia!" Newport roared. "The course is due west!"

But on the flagship the silence grew heavy. There was no doubt about it now; they were lost. Another day and night; more soundings; no bottom. Would they ever find land? Perhaps Captain Ratcliffe had been right; perhaps they should turn back while they had enough food to get back. Perhaps . . .

At dawn, the morning of the twenty-sixth of April, a voice sang out, "Land ho-o-o-o!"

They had found Virginia! Men yelled and laughed and stamped. They scrambled to the ratlines, hungry for the sight of land. Gradually the shadow of the western horizon took shape—a low, sandy coast line, with green trees.

At noon Captain Newport shot the sun and passed the good word. They were in the latitude of the Chesapeake Bay. A breeze brought them the tangy scent of pines and the perfume of flowers. The men cheered wildly. All anger, all impatience, disappeared.

Two leadsmen in the chains sounded constantly as they felt their way toward shore. A cry warned them. "Shoal water!"

Captain Newport ordered the ships to come to anchor, and put out boats to explore the land.

"Let me go! Oh, please let me go!" David begged silently, but when the boats spurted toward the shore, they left him on deck.

Old Tim saw his disappointment. "You'll get your turn, Davy." He handed him a spyglass. "Here, lad, you can look at the land. This'll bring it so close you'll think you are there."

"Thank you, Tim!" David swallowed his disappointment and climbed to a perch where he could watch the shore. He saw the men leap from the boats; some knelt to scoop a handful of earth; one man did what David wanted to do—knelt and laid his face against the ground.

Suddenly David gasped and almost dropped the glass. From the woodland behind the beach he saw Indians, with bows and arrows in their mouths, creeping silently toward the white men.

CHAPTER FOUR

By Order of the London Company

"INDIANS!" DAVID tried to yell, but he only croaked.

Before he could find his voice, the painted savages leaped to their feet, yelling, and attacked. For a moment there was a confused scramble. Then two muskets barked, and the Indians whirled and disappeared.

Shaking, David watched through the glass as the white men hurried toward their boats. A sailor staggered and fell. Two men carried him. Captain Archer was weaving on his feet, too. He was holding out both hands; blood ran down and stained the sand. A man offered his arm, but Captain Archer shook his head and kept walking.

Soon the boats that had carried gay, shouting men to the shore brought back their silent loads. On the flagship, men were silent, too. Some were shaking; one leaned on the rail and retched.

They laid the wounded sailor on the deck and covered him with a blanket; though his face glistened with sweat, he shivered.

Dr. Wotten knelt to examine him. "Start giving him brandy." He turned to Captain Archer, who stood, his feet widespread, watching the blood from his hands *splat-splat* on the deck. The doctor said, "Good thing they are bleeding—in case the arrows were poisoned."

David gasped. "Poisoned?"

"They may be," Dr. Wotten said. "Some savage tribes use them. The least little prick, and a man dies of tetanus."

David swallowed hard. "How can you tell?"

Captain Archer smiled grimly. "If I don't die of lock-jaw, the arrows weren't poisoned."

Dr. Wotten jerked a nod toward the galley. "Heat an iron. White hot." He nodded toward Archer. "Start giving him brandy, too."

Archer's eyes widened. "What are you going to do?"

"Cauterize your wounds. Better to be on the safe side."

"Will that save me, if the arrows were poisoned?"

Dr. Wotten hesitated, then shrugged. "We don't know. It may help." He called to the galley. "I want that iron white hot! Do you hear me, there?"

Archer flinched and tried to joke. "Sounds as though the cure is worse than the wound."

The doctor did not smile. "Ever see a man die of lock-jaw?"

From the galley a voice yelled, "Ready!"

Dr. Wotten knelt by the sailor. "Hold him."

Four men grabbed his arms and legs and pinned him to the deck. A man ran from the galley with a white-hot iron. David turned away. He heard a gasp, then a hoarse, animal cry. He smelled burned flesh and fled to the rail.

Old Tim joined him there. "Too bad to hurt him that way. He isn't going to live. . . . Had about enough adventuring, lad?"

David set his teeth and shook his head.

That evening, Master Hunt prayed:

"Almighty God, who art a strong tower of defense unto thy servants against the face of their enemies, we yield thee prayer and thanksgiving for our deliverance . . ."

Heartsick, David listened. How many times, he wondered, would they hear that prayer? How many times would men die in a sudden Indian attack? Was this what had happened to the lost colony of Roanoke? Were the men and women going about their work, and the children playing, and all at once yells from the forest and the hiss of arrows? Had they all been killed quickly, or had some of them . . .

He felt Tim's eyes on him, and tried to think of something else. Tonight, they would open the closed, sealed box, and know the names of the Virginia Council. He tried to think of the box.

That night on the flagship lanterns lighted the scene; on the poop deck, the three masters of the ships sat around a table that held the closed, sealed box. The gentlemen from all three ships crowded the deck of the *Susan Constant*. The crew of the *Susan* climbed on the fo'c'sle to listen. Guards brought John Smith, still in chains, to the flagship.

Mr. Wingfield shouted, "No! I say *no!* A mutineer has no place in this meeting!"

Captain Newport's stare was long and level. "Mr. Wingfield, I am still in charge." He laid his hand on the box. "Even after this box is opened, I am still in charge until we have chosen the site for our settlement." He broke the seal, opened the box, and picked up a sheet of parchment. "The names of the Virginia Council. Your name, Mr. Wingfield, naturally heads the list."

Captain Ratcliffe's hooded eyes narrowed. "Why *naturally?*"

Mr. Wingfield mounted the stairs to the poop. "I am the only member of the original London Company who has come to Virginia! They would hardly omit my name from the council!"

"I suppose," Ratcliffe said, "you know the names of the rest of the council, too."

"I do not! But I do know this! The men of the council were carefully chosen, by men of sound judgment. All right, Newport, you may continue."

Captain Newport read, " 'Captain Bartholomew Gosnold, Captain John Ratcliffe, and Captain Christopher Newport.' "

Wingfield nodded. "Naturally."

Newport continued, " 'Captain John Martin.' "

David craned his neck and saw a slim, rather frail-looking man join the others on the poop.

"An excellent choice," Mr. Wingfield said. "Captain

44

Martin's forebears were goldsmiths. When we find gold-bearing ore—"

Newport read, " 'Captain George Kendall.' "

A swarthy man with a hawk face took the steps two at a time and swaggered to the table.

Wingfield nodded. "A man of spirit. As I said, the London Company are men of excellent judgment. Excellent."

Newport looked up from the parchment. "And one more name. Captain John Smith."

"No!" Wingfield shrilled. "No! I absolutely refuse to have a mutineer seated on—"

"Mr. Wingfield," Newport said, "I am still in charge." He paused. Not even the sound of breathing broke the stillness. "John Smith shall not be seated." He picked up another paper. "I'll now read our directions for colonizing."

From where he stood between two guards John Smith said, "One request, Captain Newport. If I don't understand anything about our instructions, may I ask questions?"

"You may." Newport scanned the paper and glanced up. "We are to settle on a navigable river. Preferably one that bears to the north and west. That will help us to reach a route to the China Sea more quickly. We are not to settle near the mouth of a river. Too much danger from attack by the Spanish. And they advise . . ." He looked down at the paper, frowned, then began to read slowly: " 'Do not let the natives inhabit between you and the coast.' "

Captain Smith cocked his head. "A question, please. Do the gentlemen of London explain how we can do that? If we go up a navigable river, won't we find Indian villages dotting the banks, all the way to the coast?"

Newport did not answer. He read: " 'Try not to offend the natives.' "

The men who had been ashore that afternoon muttered. Captain Archer looked at his bandaged hands.

Newport looked up and spoke quickly. "We are not to let the natives know we intend to make a permanent settlement—not until we are well established."

Again John Smith cocked his head. "A question, please. We are to make friends with them—not to offend them. But we are to begin by telling them lies. Do the gentlemen from London explain how we can carry out both orders?"

Newport's smile was wry. "No, Captain Smith. Perhaps you have a suggestion?"

"I have!" John Smith barked. "I say—deal fairly—but sternly—from the beginning! We have what they want and need! Copper and iron! I say—trade with them for land to settle! Trade with them for corn to plant! Tell the truth, deal fairly, and be ready to fight at the drop of a hat! I say—"

Wingfield hammered the table. "That's enough! The settlement of Virginia is not going to be *your* concern! Go on, Newport!"

Newport continued. " 'Do not settle in thick woods. Do not settle on low and moist land. Do not . . .' " He read on and on.

When he paused for a moment men began to argue; the arguments rose to shouts.

"Silence!" Newport bellowed. He began to read again. " 'Lastly and chiefly, the way to prosper and achieve good success is to make yourselves all of one mind.' " His level stare swept the crowd of muttering men. Again his smile was wry. " *'All of one mind.'* They don't say how to achieve that, either."

The next morning on the *Susan*, they opened the hatches and brought out a boat that had been stored in sections, ready to put together. By evening, it was ready—a sturdy shallop, with one mast, two sails, and oars to handle it when the wind was against them.

The following day Newport sent a crew to sound for a channel into the great river that flowed into the bay. When the captain nodded at him, David could feel his grin spread from ear to ear.

"We'll find a channel in jig time!" Red declared. "This river's nigh four miles wide."

"Maybe," Tim said, "and maybe not. Sometimes water is spread mighty thin."

Red laughed as they shoved off. The leadsman laughed, too, as he made the first cast. Then he stopped laughing. The lead had scarcely disappeared when the line stopped running out. A sand bar.

All morning they sweated at the oars, and the leadsman cast time and again. Sand bars and shallows everywhere. No channel deep enough for their ships. The sun rose, reached its zenith, and beat down. The crew began to mutter. It was midafternoon when they approached a point of land on the north bank of the river. Was it any use to sound there? Probably not . . . but they cast. . . .

Deep water! Back to the ship they sped, shouting, "A channel! A channel! Close by that point of land!"

Red wiped his dripping face and bellowed, "It gave us good comfort, I can tell you!"

Newport shouted back through his trumpet. "Then we'll call it 'Point Comfort'! All right, Mr. Hodges! Weigh anchor!"

Men cheered as they leaned on the capstan bars; they laughed as they lay aloft. The waiting was over! The three ships entered the channel and anchored off Point Comfort.

A group of Indians appeared on the riverbank, and lifted their hands in greeting.

Captain Newport said, "Man a boat, Mr. Hodges. We'll go ashore and parley with them."

There was a moment of silence on the flagship. Men looked at each other and lowered their eyes quickly. Were they remembering their first time ashore?

Captain Newport must have sensed the mood. He smiled grimly. "Ask for volunteers, Mr. Hodges."

David stepped forward instantly.

Red grinned. "Can't let the younker go alone, can we, Tim?"

He and Tim stepped forward, too. Soon the boat was manned with sailors and loaded with gentlemen.

Captain Newport said, "Light all matches and keep them lighted."

One gentleman was holding a small coil of lightweight rope, with fire smoldering on one end. He passed it along, and every man lighted his own coil, blowing on the tip of rope until it smoldered. When all matches were lighted, Newport signaled, and the boat put in to shore.

One of the Indians stepped forward. "Greetings, white men!"

"He speaks English!" Newport's eyes brightened. "He must have known the colony at Roanoke!"

But the Indian said he had never been to the south; he had never known white men; he had learned his white-man words from an Indian who had died years ago. He could not tell them of white men to the south, but he could be their talker-between.

"Greetings, Talker-Between!" Newport said. "What tribe is this? Who is your chieftain?"

They were the Kecoughtans, Talker-Between told them; they called their chieftain The Kecoughtan. "Come! He waits to greet you!" He started through the forest.

The white men followed. The other Indians, closing in behind the white men, followed silently. David swallowed and found his tongue was dry. Was this a trap? Or were the Kecoughtans going to be friendly?

They reached a high stockade, made of logs standing upright, laced together with some sort of tough branches. At the gate, more Indians waited, and motioned them to come inside. David clenched his fists to try to stop the trembling of his hands. They entered the stockade.

Inside the stockade he saw Indian houses, long and narrow, shaped like an arbor, and covered with overlap-

49

ping rows of bark. Some were no larger than a small room; some were as big as a meetinghouse.

In the center of the village they found The Kecoughtan, seated on a high, bedlike throne, with painted warriors behind him. He, too, greeted them as friends; his people spread a feast of meat, fish, and berries. They sang and danced for the white men.

After the feasting, Newport began to ask questions. "Tell us about the rivers that flow into the Chesapeake Bay."

The Kecoughtan drew a map in the sand, and Talker-Between explained. This first great river, where they were now, was the Powhatan. Next was the Pamunkey, then the Rappahannock, and the Potomac. That other great river, far to the north, was the Susquehanna.

"That's it!" one whispered. "See how it bears to the north and the west!"

Newport did not answer. He only studied the map in the sand.

Back on the *Susan Constant* that night, the men argued loud and long.

They should go north up the bay, and find the Susquehanna. They'd have a better chance of finding the route to the China Sea.

But Newport shook his head. "We are months behind schedule. We must locate our settlement and get a crop in."

The next morning the shallop and the longboat from the *Susan Constant*, with Newport and Gosnold in command, started up the Powhatan to sound for a channel and choose the site for their settlement.

On the flagship, some of the men muttered, but most of them cheered. The long waiting was almost over. In a day or two the boats would be back.

That night David stood on deck, watching the sun blaze a golden path down the river. When darkness fell, he stretched out on the deck to sleep. The black sky glittered with stars. A whippoorwill's eerie cry threaded the silence; an owl's hoot shivered and died. He breathed deep of the scent of pine and the fragrance of flowers. "Earth's only paradise." That was what George Percy had called Virginia. David smiled in the darkness. He could not have thought of something like that to say, but he knew what George Percy meant. It was a good land! Tomorrow, or the next day, when they went ashore to make their new home . . .

More than a week passed before the longboat returned to pilot them up the river. The crew shook their heads. What a river! The channel twisted and turned like a snake! The ships weighed anchor and started up the river. Light, fitful winds slowed their speed to a crawl.

When they reached the place chosen for their settlement, there was no sign of the shallop; no sign of her crew. What had happened? On up the river they crawled.

At last they sighted the shallop; Newport and Gosnold came aboard the *Susan Constant*, shaking their heads. The spot they had chosen would not do; an Indian village too near. They must search further.

The men cast longing looks toward the shore. Fourteen days now since they had first landed; when would they get settled? On up the muddy river they crawled, sounding for the channel, searching the banks for a likely spot.

Fifteen days . . . sixteen days. . . . Toward noon of the seventeenth day Captain Newport hailed the shallop and motioned toward a peninsula jutting out from the north bank of the river. "Sound there for a mooring."

"Aye, aye, sir!" The answer was flat with despair. The weary crew headed toward the peninsula.

Gosnold and Ratcliffe came aboard the *Susan* with their spyglasses. Mr. Wingfield joined the captains on the poop.

"Well," he said, "have we found our spot at last?"

Newport studied the peninsula through his glass. "If the water is deep enough for our ships." He handed his glass to Wingfield.

The gray-bearded man studied the land. "Excellent!" His thin voice was shrill with excitement. "An ideal spot! Almost an island! Just a narrow neck of land connecting it to the shore. We can protect ourselves from attack very easily."

Captain Gosnold lowered his glass and shook his head. "It's too heavily wooded."

A yell came for the crew of the shallop. "Deep water!"

Newport lifted his trumpet. "How deep?"

"Six fathoms! Our ships can ride at anchor in six fathoms, moored to the trees!"

"This is it!" Newport said.

Gosnold pleaded, "Captain Newport! It's low! It's marshy! It's heavily wooded! We were warned about all those things! We were warned not to be in a hurry to settle!"

Newport scowled. "When the London Company said

'don't be in a hurry to settle,' they expected us to be in Virginia before the end of January. Man alive, it's the middle of May! We've got to get settled! This is the best spot we've found! It's easily fortified—we can see up and down the river—"

"Please, Captain Newport—"

But Newport lifted his trumpet in one hand and pointed with the other toward the peninsula. "This is James Island!" he shouted. "This is where Jamestown will be! Pass the word!"

Captain Gosnold's lips moved again, pleading, but the cheers drowned his words.

CHAPTER FIVE

The Trial of John Smith

CHEERING and shouting, they moored the ships to the trees of James Island, and landed. Even John Smith—freed of his chains, but still under guard—was allowed ashore.

Captain Newport shouted his first order with a smile. "I want three groups of volunteers to search for springs of good, clear water."

Cheering still, the men volunteered and scattered to search. At dusk, when they returned, none had found a spring, but they were still in high spirits. Tomorrow, or the next day, they would find springs. What a land!

That night the council—all but John Smith—elected Mr.

Wingfield president. Before a mass meeting Master Hunt administered the oath. When the solemn words ended, President Wingfield thrust out his bearded chin and cast a stern look about him.

"As president of the Virginia Council, my first demand is that John Smith be kept in chains until Captain Newport sails. And that he—"

Captain Newport interrupted quietly. "According to our laws, President Wingfield, you cannot demand. You can only suggest. The council must vote on all measures. You have two votes; the rest of the council have one vote each; but that is the limit of your power."

President Wingfield subsided, muttering.

Newport went on. "Before we vote, I have one suggestion. My orders are to explore for a route to the China Sea. John Smith is an experienced navigator, and a good surveyor and maker of maps. I'd like to take him with me on that exploration."

The men of the council nodded; they voted, five to two, that John Smith should accompany Captain Newport on his exploration.

"Very well!" Wingfield said. "You're responsible for him, Newport! And when you return to England, he goes back with you, to stand trial for plotting mutiny!"

John Smith said nothing. He cocked an eyebrow, studied Wingfield, shrugged, and strolled away.

David followed and found him standing looking across the wide, tawny river. "I'm glad, sir, that you're going to get to explore with Captain Newport."

"Thank you, David."

"And—and I'm glad President Wingfield doesn't have the final say about things!"

John Smith wheeled and glared at him. "Oh, you are, are you? You think it's a good thing to set up a president with no power? Of all the idiotic ways to plan a colony! In any emergency situation, the man in charge must have power! And this, my little gentleman, is going to be an emergency situation! *The president can only suggest!* Balderdash!"

"But—but—if he could command, look what would happen to you! If—"

"Stop thinking about one man!" John Smith roared. "Think about this settlement! *The president can only suggest!* Heaven help this colony!"

"But, sir—"

"Don't babble about what you don't know about!"

"Very good, sir!" And David stamped off, simmering.

The next morning the council divided the men into groups and put them to work. The laborers toiled; the gentlemen strolled about and gave orders.

Toward afternoon, President Wingfield's plan for Jamestown began to take shape. Men had paced off a triangle to enclose the town. Now, as workmen felled trees and stripped them, others piled the branches, higgledy-piggledy, along the sides of the triangle. Some of the men argued against this method of "fortifying" Jamestown.

"There is no need to build a fort!" Wingfield insisted. "We are commanded not to offend the natives!"

John Smith roared, "We were not commanded to show weakness before them! I say—build a fort! I say—"

"Your orders," Wingfield shouted, "are to explore with Captain Newport! You are not in charge of the building of Jamestown!"

"So much the worse for Jamestown!" John Smith bellowed, and he strode on board the *Discovery*, where David was helping to ready her for the voyage of exploration.

David set his jaw and stuck at his work. Before he'd say anything to that man again . . . But John Smith strode over and stood by him. David stiffened, and touched his forelock.

"I've told Captain Newport you'll be a good man for our crew, David."

The cold knot of anger melted, and David grinned. "Thank you!"

"*Sir!*" John Smith barked.

"*Sir!*" He didn't risk saying anything else.

Four days later, the *Discovery* weighed anchor for her trip to explore up the river. When David heard the command, "Topmen into the rigging!" he smiled as he climbed. *A good man for our crew*, the captain had said, and he had John Smith to thank for it that he was a good man for the crew. Some day, David thought, I'll tell him . . . No, I won't, either! Almost every time I speak to him he makes me so mad . . .

A mighty cheer banished his thoughts about John Smith. Captain Newport was on the poop, waiting till the cheers died down, so he could address his company.

"You gentlemen," he said, "will go down in history with Gilbert, Raleigh, and Frobisher; with Hawkins, and Davis, and Drake. For you are going to succeed in doing what Englishmen have tried to do for over a hundred years! You are going to find a new route to the China Sea!"

Cheers echoed; even Newport smiled.

"You know how many times Englishmen searched for a passage in the far north; ice blocked our way. You know that Spain and Portugal hold the passages to the south, around Cape Horn and the Cape of Good Hope. You know that Spain holds the overland route, from Nombre de Dios to Panama. For long years she has barred us from the riches of Cathay. But that time is over! Now we shall find another overland route, like the route across Panama!"

Louder cheers.

"I do not know just how far it is from the Atlantic to the Pacific Ocean here. Perhaps it is a bit further than across the Isthmus of Panama; perhaps not so far. But, before we return to Jamestown, we'll find the headwaters of this river! We'll cross the mountains and see before us the westward-flowing river! We'll find an English route to all the riches of Cathay!"

The men yelled themselves hoarse. From that moment on, they cheered everything. There were no arguments, no disputes, no huddling in groups and muttering. They were brothers, under one leader, going ahead with one purpose.

Up the river they sailed, visiting Indian villages. Soon they had picked up enough Indian words to ask questions. Was there great salt water to the west? Yes, the Indians told them, great salt water.

Well up the river they saw the smoke of an Indian village on a high bluff on the north bank. When they went ashore, the chieftain of the village received them. He was Powhatan, he told them—not the great Powhatan, ruler of many tribes, but his brother, the little Powhatan.

Was there great salt water to the west? they asked him.

The chieftain said he did not know. His enemies, the Monacans, lived to the west. His people did not go further west. The white men must not go further west, either. It would make trouble for the Powhatans.

Newport tried to explain; the white men came as friends; they were friends of the Powhatans; they would be friends of the Monacans, too.

The chieftain raised a clenched fist and shouted. They must not go further west!

Newport did not answer that. He planted a cross on the high bluff; he renamed the Powhatan River the James, and took possession in the name of King James of England.

Back on the *Discovery*, he said, "We sail on!"

His men cheered. The gay mood lasted until they began to hear a vast, hollow roar, as though the father of all storms was raging through the forest, sweeping down upon them. The waters of the James grew deeper and swifter, with sudden whirlpools. The vast, hollow roar grew louder. Then they found the reason. Ahead of them, the river plunged down over huge boulders in thundering falls.

Stunned, the men gaped at the sight, and turned to their captain.

For a long time Newport studied the frowning cliffs, the mighty boulders. At last he shrugged. "I expected a rise in the land," he admitted, "but nothing like this. I cannot spare the time now to explore through that sort of country." And he gave the order to return to Jamestown.

Disheartened, the men turned back. On the voyage downriver, they began muttering again.

David was off duty when they came in sight of James Island. He climbed into the ratlines for a first glimpse of Jamestown, then scampered down, and dashed to find John Smith.

"Wait till you see what's happening! You're going to feel good! They're fortifying Jamestown! Building a stockade!"

"So?" The captain had no answering smile. "Wingfield has learned his lesson. I wonder how many men died to teach him that we need a fort?"

In grim silence they moored the *Discovery* and hurried ashore to find what had happened in Jamestown.

An Indian attack had left one dead and two dozen badly wounded. The injured men were on the deck of the *Susan Constant.*

David went aboard the flagship to help care for the wounded. Some stared at him, unseeing, and babbled feverishly. Others, not so badly hurt, were conscious and muttering. Was this their paradise? Their promised land? They had not been in Virginia six weeks; already two Indian attacks; already two dead and thirty wounded. Where was the gold? Where was the route to the China Sea?

One man, with flushed face and blackened lips, begged, "Water . . . water . . ."

Another nodded toward the ship's cask. "Get him a drink, will you? It's pretty stinking, but it's better than nothing."

"Haven't you found a spring yet?" David asked.

"We haven't had time to hunt for springs!"

David gagged at the stench, but he brought the water.

Another man, with a festering wound on his leg, struggled to sit up, propped himself on his hands, and looked about groggily. "It was one of these guns on the *Susan* that scared off the Indian attack. Wonder what will happen to us after the ships go home?"

David couldn't think of an answer. He was wondering, too.

That night Captain Newport faced a mass meeting and reported on their trip up the James River. "There is no doubt that the China Sea is somewhere not far to the west; all the Indians had heard of great salt water beyond the mountains."

"Then let's go!" Wingfield said. "Let's find it! You were ordered to spend a month in exploration!"

Newport shook his head. "The London Company expected us to be in Virginia by the end of January. It's June now—almost six months since we dropped down the Thames. We're going to need supplies just as fast as I can return to England to bring them."

As always, the argument rose to shouts:

Yes! Newport should return immediately!

No! He should stay until they found gold! If they did not send back a valuable cargo, they might not get any supplies!

He must sail now!

No! He must not sail without a cargo! What would the London Company think if they got no return on their investment?

At last they decided to make clapboard to load the *Susan Constant*. That would give the investors a taste of the fine trees they had found in Virginia. It should not take long to make clapboard.

But making clapboard was easier said than done. First, they had to find the right trees, and when they did find a good tree, like as not they had to cut down three other trees before they could fell the one they wanted. The handful of laborers slaved in the murky heat. The gentlemen strolled about restlessly and urged them to work faster.

Captain Martin called for several of the best laborers to do something special for him. He did not explain what. The workmen dropped their axes, picked up shovels, and followed him and three gentlemen.

When they returned, they staggered under bags of dirt, which they loaded into a barrel. The word passed quickly. Captain Martin had found gold-bearing ore! Everyone cheered now. When the London Company saw that, all would be well!

At last the *Susan Constant* was loaded. The remaining stores for the settlers were brought ashore from the *Godspeed* and put into the storehouse. Thomas Studley, their cape merchant, in charge of supplies, checked on the stores and reported with a worried frown. Excepting for a small amount of wine, oil, beef, and ship's biscuit, there was nothing but grain.

"We'll make out," President Wingfield said. "Captain Newport should be back in ten weeks with—"

"It will take me at least twenty weeks," Newport said.

"Twenty weeks!" Wingfield's voice was shrill. "It should not take you more than four weeks to London, and six weeks for the westward crossing again!"

"Six weeks wasn't long enough for the westward crossing when we came over. It was more than four months from the time we dropped down the Thames until we sighted Virginia."

"But we were wind-bound; we had scurvy; we stopped a month in the West Indies until our sick recovered; we—"

"I may be wind-bound again," Newport said. "I promise to be back in twenty weeks, but I won't promise to be here sooner."

"But that will be the end of October!"

"Or the first week in November," Newport said. "If we sail now. The longer I stay, the later it will be."

"Then go!" President Wingfield shouted. "And take John Smith with you!"

"Why take me to London?" Captain Smith asked. "Why not try me here and now? In the open? Before all the men of Jamestown?"

"But—but—" Wingfield stammered.

"Why not?" John Smith asked. "My accusers are here."

The council looked at each other and nodded. The trial began. One after another, President Wingfield called up nine workmen; one after another, the nine men testified that John Smith had bribed them to help him in a plot: After Newport had sailed, John Smith intended to murder the council and to rule as King of Virginia.

Nine times President Wingfield said, "Well, John Smith?"

Nine times the captain answered, "I have nothing to say."

The president called his last witness—Tom Willis, another of the laborers, a scrawny little man with buck teeth and beady eyes that reminded David of a rat.

"Yes, sir," Tom Willis testified, "before we reached the Canaries, Captain Smith approached me, and bribed me to help start a mutiny."

John Smith strolled over to face the fellow. "Tom Willis, you signed on and started to Virginia without a shilling in your pocket, didn't you?"

"Aye, sir!" Tom looked very righteous. "I suppose that's why you thought I'd fall in with your dastardly plan."

"How much did I pay you when I bribed you? Be careful what you say! There are men here who know exactly what money I had with me when we sailed!"

Tom's beady eyes shifted back and forth for a moment. Then he smirked. "You didn't pay me anything, sir. You promised me a share of the gold we'd find in Virginia. After we killed the council and set you up as king."

"I paid you nothing?"

"Not a shilling, sir."

"So you reached Virginia with your purse as empty as you sailed?"

Again Tom's beady eyes shifted. At last he said, "Aye, sir. That's a fact, sir. Not a shilling to my name."

John Smith turned away. "Captain Newport, before you sail, there is one thing you should know. Some of your crew have been stealing from the stores for the return voyage and selling the food to the settlers."

President Wingfield jumped to his feet. "Don't try to change the subject! You won't escape by—"

But Newport was on his feet, too, his eyes blazing. "You can prove that charge?"

"I can. One of the thieves is ready to confess. Where is Lew Jones, from the *Godspeed?*"

A big fellow ambled forward and touched his forelock. Yes, he admitted, they had been doing a little trading on the side—selling part of their supplies to the settlers. "We didn't mean any harm, sir," he told Captain Newport. "After all, it was food for the fo'c'sle that we sold; we figured we'd get along; we've been on short rations before."

"What did you do with the food?" John Smith asked.

"Sneaked it off the ship and hid it in the woods."

"You can show Captain Newport where it is hidden?"

"Aye, aye, sir."

"What settlers bought from you?" John Smith asked.

"Just one man. Tom Willis."

Captain Smith wheeled and grabbed a handful of Tom's shirt. "Tom Willis! You've admitted you had no money when you came aboard! You've admitted I paid you no money! Where did you get the money you gave Lew Jones?"

Tom's beady eyes were wild; his head tried to crawl between his shoulders.

"Talk! Or I'll choke it out of you!"

"It was given to me," Tom gasped. "A—a—gentleman gave it to me! He said if I would get some of my friends to swear that you planned a mutiny—"

John Smith twisted his hand. His knuckles were against Tom's scrawny throat. "Who gave you the money? Who?"

"Mr. Wingfield!"

Captain Smith released his grip, gave Tom a shove that sent him spinning, turned, and hooked his thumbs in his belt. "Well, President Wingfield?"

In shocked silence the men of Jamestown stared at their president.

"*You!*" Newport gasped.

President Wingfield was haughty. "I admit my action was irregular, but my reason was sound. I never intended that John Smith should hang—just that he should be removed from the colony." His voice sharpened. "John Smith is a bragging upstart, a troublemaker and a rabble-rouser! I refuse to have him in Virginia!"

Some of the gentlemen nodded; a muttering began.

"President Wingfield," Captain Newport said, "any action requires the consent of the council."

The council marched off to Newport's cabin aboard the *Susan Constant*. In Jamestown, men gathered in hud-

dles and muttered, shooting sidelong glances at each other.

David joined Tim and Red. "Wingfield's the one that ought to go to London in chains!"

"Aye," old Tim said, "but he won't. He's a member of the original London Company. Besides, lad, half the gentlemen here agree with him."

"*What!*"

Red nodded. "Right, Tim. They don't like the captain. He's twice the man they are, and they know it. That hurts!" He chuckled. "Sort of a neat idea of Wingfield's, if he wanted to get rid of a fellow, wasn't it?"

"But—but—but—" David spluttered. He stopped.

The council had returned, stony-faced, to the meeting.

"Well, President Wingfield?" Captain Newport urged.

The president stiffened and stared over the heads of the men. "The council has voted, five to two, to seat John Smith. The council has also voted, five to two, to fine their president two hundred pounds—said fine to be paid to said John Smith."

A confusion of murmurs, cheers, and growls greeted the decision. Captain Smith stood, thumbs in his belt, one eyebrow cocked, casting a slow glance over the men of Jamestown. Finally he spoke very quietly.

"Said John Smith thanks the council for seating him, but refuses to accept the fine. Let it be paid into the general fund of the colony."

This time the cheers shouted down the mutters—but the mutters were still there.

Captain Newport yelled over the noise. "Attention! Before I sail, there is one order that must be carried out. The pinnace must be stripped of her sails and oars, and her heavy anchor. These things must be stowed on shore, under lock and key."

Captain Kendall glared. "That's an insult! As much as to tell us we'd be cowards and deserters if we had a chance!"

Newport's tone was dry. "It has happened before in the history of exploration." He shouted, "Hop to it! Strip the pinnace!"

David saw Bert and Jem aboard the *Godspeed* and joined them.

Bert's mouth twisted in a half smile. "Signing on the *Godspeed*, too, are you? Came to your senses, the same as we did?"

David stared. "You mean you're not staying in Virginia?"

"Ah!" Bert snarled. "A pack of lies they told us about Virginia! It's just the same as England for the likes of us. Work, work, work, and the gentlemen stand around and give orders! I'm going home! I may never own a house, but I'll have a better place to live than anything in Jamestown! Ship's fare ain't much, but it's better than the food they'll eat in Jamestown! No, sir! Jem and me—we're going home—same as you!"

"But I'm not going," David said.

Jem stared. "But—but—Master Davy!"

Bert's lip curled in a sneer. "Probably brought up to think 'a Warren can't desert his post'!" With a short laugh, he wheeled. "Come along, Jem, let's stow our gear."

Jem was still looking at David with a puzzled frown. At last, he straightened. "I'm staying, too."

"What!" Bert bellowed.

Jem laid his big hand on David's shoulder, and for once his fingers were not biting in. He smiled down at David, and there was no mockery in his eyes. "You see, Bert, I've always looked after this lad. So if he's staying, I'm staying, too."

"Why—you—you—"

"Come along, Master Davy."

Jem and David left the *Godspeed* together.

"Do you think they'll let me stay, Master Davy?"

"Once," David said, "you called me just *Davy*. I liked that."

"You did?" Jem grinned. "Then Davy it is!" He gripped David's shoulder. "Say, five months before the mast sort of muscled you up!"

"And look at my hands! They aren't real clean yet!"

They laughed together.

Jem asked again, "Do you think they'll let me stay?"

"We'll talk to Captain Smith," David promised. "He's a friend of mine."

John Smith listened to Jem. His lips quirked. He looked at David. "So you told Jem I was a friend of yours?"

David met the captain's gaze squarely. "Yes, sir. Because you dared me to sail before the mast. You made me so blamed mad I did it. And that toughened me up. I can hand, reef, and steer pretty well. And I can eat anything that holds still!"

John Smith threw back his head and shouted with laughter. Still smiling, he looked at Jem. "And you want to stay in Jamestown? Good! We can do with more men like you."

Jem's dark face was shining. "Thank you, sir!"

David grinned. "We'll both try to be worth our quarter of a ton of supplies."

The captain's smile disappeared. His voice was harsh. "We don't have those supplies now, David. We're going to be on short rations—every man of us! Better think twice, both of you, before you decide to stay." And he strode off, leaving Jem and David alone in a silence that stretched.

They looked at each other.

"You really want to stay, Davy? You're set on it?"

"Yes. But you don't have to stay, Jem. If you—"

"Of course I'm staying!" He looked about at the little fort between the wide, tawny river and the endless forest. His eyes were troubled. At last he shook his head quickly, as though to banish his thoughts. "We'll get along all right, Davy! We'll get along!" But his eyes were still troubled.

CHAPTER SIX

"Hide Your Losses from the Indians"

THE next day, on the ebb tide, the two ships sailed. Slowly at first, then more swiftly, they dropped down the James and disappeared. There was nothing left now but the little fort between the vast river and the forest.

All day a silence hung over Jamestown. Men talked in mutters and answered with shrugs. The last tie with home was gone; anything they did not have in the fort—anything they could not get from the forest or the river—they must do without until Newport could go and come again across three thousand miles of ocean. And ships could be wind-bound; men could die of scurvy; sudden storms could wreck the stoutest ship . . . So the men of Jamestown were silent.

Once more President Wingfield sent men out to search for a spring of fresh water; once more the men returned with bad news. There were no springs on James Island.

"Then we'll have to drink the water of the river," their president said.

They drew buckets; muddy—but it would be all right when it had settled. One man was too thirsty to wait for the water to settle. He dipped a cup, drank, and spat it out.

"Salty as brine!"

They could not believe. Others tasted, and spat it out, too. They stared at each other. Were they marooned, with no fresh water?

One man laughed. "The tide! That is all! When the tide is in, of course the water will be salty!"

The man smiled at themselves. That was it. They would wait until the tide went out, and then fill their water casks with fresh water! They were cheerful about it—until they filled the casks. With the ebbing tide, the water was slimy with mud. Even after it settled and grew tepid, it was still brackish.

Jem drank, made a face, then grinned. "Nasty, but it won't kill us!"

The others laughed, too, and slapped him on the shoulder. They liked the big fellow.

Jem said the same thing about the mosquitoes, too, when they came in whining swarms and tortured their sleep. "Nasty, but they won't kill us!"

The others did not laugh with him about the mosquitoes, but at least they could smile. Jem was right; the water was bad, and the mosquitoes were a nuisance, but bad water and mosquitoes would not kill them!

Perhaps they were not very comfortable, but at least they were safe. They had a good, stout palisade with bulwarks shaped like half-moons at the three corners and demi-culverins mounted there, ready to pour shot on invaders. No ship could surprise them without warning. And no Indians could reach them by a sudden rush from the mainland, either. More cannon commanded the narrow neck of land to the shore. What if their supply was down to nothing but barley and wheat? They could hunt and fish, couldn't they? Every morning they could send their best marksmen to the forest on the mainland to hunt. With plenty of fresh meat . . .

But soon the game disappeared from the forest near Jamestown. One day, three hunters, ranging further into the forest, did not return. The next morning, a search party went out to find them and returned, white-lipped.

They had found the three hunters—dead—each with an arrow in his back. They had buried the three in the forest, and smoothed the graves. They were supposed to hide any deaths from the Indians. Not that they could hide those deaths. The Indians knew.

Captain Kendall's dark eyes blazed. "I wish I'd been there when those painted devils—"

John Smith said, "Four graves, instead of three? That would not help."

Kendall flushed. "At least," he said, "our fort is safe! Nothing can enter the palisade without getting a taste of our guns!"

And nothing did enter—excepting the heat—and the whining mosquitoes. But the July sun beat down on the low island; heat rose from the swampland in a muggy mist. Men, trying to work, panted and tore off their hot clothes, then burned and blistered and could not sleep.

Mr. Studley, their cape merchant, took David with him to check their stores. When they had tallied the barrels of grain, Mr. Studley did a bit of figuring, then stared at David as though he had seen a ghost.

"Mr. Studley, sir, what is it? What's wrong?"

"We . . . we'd better call a meeting."

President Wingfield summoned the men, and Mr. Studley gave them the grim news. They had been depending too heavily on their store of grain. "Even if Captain Newport gets back with supplies the end of October, we must ration ourselves, or we'll starve."

"Ration ourselves?" one shouted. "More than we have?"

Mr. Studley looked heartsick. "We have not even begun to ration ourselves. From now on, it's half a pint of wheat and half a pint of barley for each man, boiled up in the common kettle, and ladled out, so each man gets his share."

"Only that, three times a day?"

"Only that," Mr. Studley said, "once a day. Otherwise, we'll starve before Newport's return."

David's scalp crawled as he felt the panic race through the men.

"We'll have to fish more," Captain Gosnold said.

One of the gentlemen sniffed. "I don't like fish."

"You'll learn to like it." Captain Gosnold was grim. "I've seen men hungry enough to wolf it raw!"

Toward the end of July, the fever struck, and men began to die. One . . . then two . . . then another. Arguments rose to a shout. It was the food! They had to have better food! It was the swamp fever! Everyone knew that swamp mist was deadly!

Sudden thunderstorms rose; lightning glared and crackled around them; thunder echoed; a deluge of rain beat their rotten tents to shreds. And always, the high, spiteful whine of mosquitoes.

"Nasty," Jem said again, "but they can't kill us."

Fever swept the town. Half the men lay burning and shivering. Of the council, only Bartholomew Gosnold and John Smith were on their feet. They were everywhere, helping Dr. Wotten care for the sick, helping dig graves when the men died.

Master Hunt was everywhere, too, giving a last communion, saying a last prayer over a man Dr. Wotten could not save. Again and again David heard the prayer:

. . . we do humbly commend the soul of this our dear brother unto thy hands . . .

Each night they buried the dead, secretly, and smoothed the graves, that the Indians might not know how many men they had lost. Each night, by the new graves, Master Hunt read the service:

". . . Man, that is born of woman, hath but a short time to live and is full of misery. He cometh up and is cut down like a flower. He fleeth as it were before a shadow . . ."

Every morning, Jem wakened David with a little shake. "Davy? You all right?" His eyes no longer mocked.

"I'm fine!" David always declared.

But one morning he wakened shaking with chills and begging for water. Dimly he remembered that Jem washed him and fanned him. Then his memories were a confusion of old days in England, his days before the mast, and the weeks in the West Indies.

It was night when the fever broke; David wakened from a dream of Christmas. Jem was beside him, in the dark, singing softly "The Coventry Carol":

> "Lul-lay, Thou little tiny Child!
> By, by, lully, lul-lay . . ."

The song whispered to silence. There was no sound but the plaint of a whippoorwill and the high whine of mosquitoes. Then David heard the *shush-shush* of footsteps, shuffling away from their hut. Men had been listening to Jem's song.

The next day David was almost too weak to stand, but with Jem's help he got on his feet and went outside. Anything, he thought, was better than staying in the dank little hovels they called houses. In England, even their animals had better shelter than this!

He shuffled through the door and stood a moment, leaning against the cabin. From across the town, he heard someone shouting.

"What's that?" he asked.

Jem grinned. "Captain Smith, probably. Trying to get some work done. Better not let him see you, or he'll put you to work, too."

77

They walked toward the sound. It was John Smith, raging at a man who was sitting in the sun, propped against the palisade. The fellow was pale and gaunt, and his hands were shaking. But John Smith bellowed at him. "So you're sick! So is everyone! But we've got to get these cabins done! We've got to have more shelter! On your feet, before I lift you with the toe of my boot!"

The fellow muttered, pulled himself to his feet, and shuffled away.

David glared at John Smith's back. "Why—that—that—" Anger stopped his words.

Jem grinned again. "I thought he was a friend of yours?"

"No man that mean is a friend to anyone!"

Jem shrugged. "We've got to have more shelter. Someone has to keep them moving. And no one can say Captain Smith tells a man to do what he won't do himself. He's working twice as hard as anyone else."

"I suppose that's right," David admitted.

But every morning when he wakened to the sound of John Smith's bellow, he was angry again for the poor, half-sick men the captain was driving to work.

Then one morning a strange silence hung over the fort. John Smith was not bellowing. Startled, David hurried to the captain's hut, and found him lying on his bunk, glassy-eyed, muttering.

David did not stop running until he found Captain Gosnold. "Captain Smith!" he gasped. "He's awfully sick!"

"Good!" someone snarled. "Now he'll find out what it's like!"

Captain Gosnold and Dr. Wotten hurried to John Smith's cabin. A moment later, Gosnold came out. "David, get Master Hunt."

His heart hammering, his mouth dry, David ran to find the minister. When Master Hunt entered the cabin, David waited outside and heard the prayer:

. . . we humbly commend this our dear brother unto thy hands . . .

The doctor did not think John Smith would get well. David crouched by the cabin, shivering, and tried to pray, and could find no words.

But four days later John Smith staggered through the door, braced his hand against the wall to steady himself, and glared about him. His voice still carried. "You, there! Why isn't that cabin done?"

Toward the end of August all building stopped. There were not enough men on their feet to take care of the sick.

One morning, Captain Gosnold did not get up. That night, he was dead. For once men forgot their panic, forgot themselves, and spoke only of him. They disregarded the orders about secret burial to hide their losses from the Indians. They buried him with full honors and fired a volley over his grave.

Tough sailors, haughty gentlemen, and hard-bitten soldiers stood with bowed heads. Many wiped away tears. John Smith stood motionless, chin up, his eyes bleak. When the service ended, he said, "I'll take his watch tonight." He strode quickly away.

David's anger boiled again. Didn't John Smith feel anything?

A few mornings later, David wakened to find Jem tossing and muttering.

Dr. Wotten came, took one look, and said, "Another of the quick ones. Get Master Hunt!"

"No, no, no!" David pleaded. "Jem isn't going to die! Jem can't die!"

But before night, Jem was dead.

David fled to John Smith's cabin, and lurched through the door, shuddering. "Jem's dead! Jem!"

The captain jumped to his feet and turned. David stumbled toward him. He had a fleeting memory of once, when he was ten—big enough to be ashamed of it—leaning against his father and sobbing. Tonight, he was not ashamed. And John Smith was the only man . . .

The captain lifted his hand. Two stinging slaps jerked David to a halt. Then the captain's hands were on his shoulders. "You all right now? Then take Jem's watch tonight. When your best friend dies, it helps to take his watch."

CHAPTER SEVEN

"Do Not Offend the Natives"

AUGUST ended; September began. Still the starving men sickened and died. Thomas Studley died. President Wingfield appointed John Smith cape merchant in his stead. David went with the captain to take tally of what was left of their stores.

Inside the storehouse, John Smith looked about. "The casks that were in this corner—where are they?"

"We didn't count them before," David said. "Just the barrels of grain. I remember Mr. Studley said there was a little oil, beef, wine, and ship's biscuit there."

"Hmmm." That was all John Smith said. They checked the grain and left the storehouse. Outside the door, John

Smith paused and looked across the way, where President Wingfield was talking to Captain Kendall. A skeleton-thin man nearby was looking toward Wingfield, too.

"Odd that our president doesn't lose weight like the rest of us!" the man said. "He is holding up remarkably well, isn't he?"

John Smith did not seem to hear. "Where is Captain Ratcliffe?" he asked.

A short time later David saw Ratcliffe, Martin, and John Smith enter the storehouse together. That afternoon the men of Jamestown came together for a mass meeting.

Wingfield was impatient. "Come, come! What is this all about? I called no meeting!"

"The rest of the council did." John Smith spoke very quietly. "President Wingfield, there were certain kegs in the storehouse: beef, oil, wine, ship's biscuit. They are not there now. The men suspect you of hiding the stores and using them for yourself."

Wingfield stiffened, glaring at the surviving members of the council. "You stand there—you men of my own council—and accuse your president of trying to save himself at the expense of others?"

"We are not accusing you," Captain Smith said. "We are asking you. Did you remove the special food from the storehouse?"

"Things have come to a pretty pass," Wingfield fumed, "when the council listens to rumors of the common herd!"

"You removed no stores?"

"Well, yes, I did," Wingfield admitted, "but only to save things for the very sick."

Captain Martin raised his haggard face. "I don't remember having any special food when I was sick."

Wingfield did not answer.

Martin's voice grew harsher. "Who has been sick enough to deserve the special food? Who?"

Still no answer. The men of the council hammered their questions now:

"Who got the food?"

"Men have been dying. Who was sick enough for the special food?"

"Where is the record of what was put in the storehouse?"

Their president did answer that question. "There is no record. That was Thomas Studley's job. He was cape merchant. It was up to him to know what was in the storehouse."

"Thomas Studley is dead."

President Wingfield spoke quickly again. "And he left no record of what he put in the storehouse, or of what he removed! Things have been carelessly handled! Very carelessly! When . . ." Their president talked on, but the men of Jamestown were not listening. They stirred restlessly and muttered. The men of the council looked at each other; they nodded toward Ratcliffe.

Captain Ratcliffe spoke for them. "Mr. Wingfield, by order of the council, you are deposed and under arrest. I have been elected president to succeed you."

Wingfield threw out his hands in a hopeless gesture. "If another man can do better than I have done, he is welcome to try!"

They marched him off to the pinnace, to live there, under arrest. Master Hunt administered the oath, and the new president of the Virginia Council lifted his hand and swore:

"I, John Ratcliffe, elected president of His Majesty's council for the first colony to Virginia . . ."

The men of Jamestown cheered and pressed around him, shaking his hand. Things would go better now!

But things did not go better; the starving men still died. Autumn came, and the murky heat gave way to a crisp tingle in the air. The sick began to feel better. If only they had food until Newport came. . . .

Then a watchman shouted, "Indians!"

The men scrambled to seize their guns, to light their matches.

The watchman shouted again. "Food! They're bringing food!"

The men dropped their guns and ran toward the gate to fling it open.

"Halt!" a voice roared.

They turned to glare at John Smith.

"As cape merchant," he said, "it is my duty to trade with the Indians!"

Alone, he walked out through the gate. A dozen tall Indians advanced with baskets of corn. One spoke enough English to make their bargain known. Food—for guns.

The men of Jamestown cheered wildly and shoved to be first through the gate with their guns.

But Captain Smith's voice rang out. "No! We have copper to trade! No guns! No swords!"

The spokesman for the Indians scowled and went back to his companions. In a moment John Smith was between two groups of angry men; the Indians shook their fists and shouted unintelligible words; the white men shouted, too:

"You fool!"

"You stubborn fool!"

"We've got to have food!"

"What is the use to hang on to swords and guns when we are starving?"

"We can't eat swords and guns, can we?"

John Smith spoke without turning. "We will not trade weapons for food."

"We will! I say we will!"

John Smith still watched the Indians. "If we start trading weapons, we are lost. They will never be satisfied with anything else."

"But we've got to have food!"

"We'll get food," he declared, "and without trading guns."

Again the Indian spokesman advanced. "We trade food for guns. No guns—no food."

Again John Smith shook his head. "We have no guns to trade."

Once more the Indians stalked away angrily. He joined his companions. They started back toward the mainland.

The mutter of the white men rose to a shout. "Rush him! Arrest him!"

John Smith wheeled to face the gate. "We will not trade guns for food!"

"You can't keep me from trading my gun!" And one man started through the gate.

John Smith leveled his musket. "I can—if I have to shoot you to do it."

David stared toward the forest, where the Indians still waited; he clenched his hands until his fingernails bit into his palms. The Indians had not gone away yet; they were still waiting for the white men to surrender.

John Smith stood like a man of bronze. He did not move or plead.

At last the spokesman came again. They would trade corn for copper.

The white men cheered hoarsely. "Food! We'll have food!"

"Silence!" John Smith bit the word through his teeth.

The trading began. He paid for the first basket of corn. The Indians set it at his feet. With a sobbing laugh, one of the white men started toward it.

The captain's scorn was a lash. "Stop! If you have to crawl, go into the fort! Crawl in front of your friends! Not before the Indians."

The man's eyes blazed with hate, but he stopped.

When the trading had ended and the Indians had gone, they ran to carry the baskets of corn and the meat into the fort. They knelt about the baskets, grabbing handfuls of corn, trying to eat it raw.

When they had made a fire, and the meat began to brown, they crouched around it, quivering, wiping the slobber from their chins. Some of them sobbed.

John Smith's face was still hard, but his eyes were sad.

Master Hunt said, "Let us give thanks that the Indians had mercy on us."

John Smith cocked an eyebrow. "You think that is why they came?"

"You!" one man shouted. "Don't you believe in anything?"

John Smith hooked his thumbs in his belt. "Certainly. I believe the Indians need copper. I believe they are as hungry for copper as we are for corn. They need metal—any metal. It must be a very tedious business, to fell trees, work logs, carve boats, without metal. I believe they have harvested their crops and have corn to trade. And I believe that if they cannot trade for guns they will trade for copper and iron! That is what I believe!"

The food the Indians had brought lasted three days. More Indians came to trade—for copper.

"A good thing," John Smith remarked, "that we did not trade for guns?"

The men did not answer.

For a time there was food. Flocks of birds, flying south, darkened the sky. The men shot birds; they fished; they even ventured into the woods and hunted. But after a few days there was no game. The sound of their guns had scared it away.

The trees turned scarlet and gold; the air grew crisp. The sickness and dying ended. Men began to smile. Newport would be back soon. They had food to last until the end of October.

With their returning strength they began to build. Their tents had rotted; there were barely enough houses to shelter the handful of survivors. They must have more houses ready when Newport came.

The stronger ones worked at felling and stripping trees; the weaker ones bound thatch for the roofs. But, work as they would, there was no chance that they could be ready with houses enough when Newport came. He might bring a hundred more settlers with him. Less than four dozen men, weakened and wasted, could not build homes for a hundred new settlers.

November came, and the first week passed. Where was Newport? Less than two weeks' store of food on hand . . .

President Ratcliffe ordered Captain Smith to take the shallop downriver, to trade for corn. "Take six men with you," he said, "so if the wind dies they can handle the boat."

"I'll need more men than that," John Smith said. "And I want soldiers—well armed."

President Ratcliffe frowned. "We are not to offend the natives. You are to trade for corn! Not to start trouble! Can I depend on that?"

"I'm going after corn," John Smith said. "And I'll get corn. I will do no more—and no less—than I must do—to get corn."

Ratcliffe hesitated, then shrugged. "Take David with you for one of your sailors. He can handle sail better than he can swing an ax."

At Kecoughtan, they lowered their sail, shipped their oars, and waited for the Indians to greet them. In May, the Kecoughtans had come to the shore, laying down their bows and arrows, holding out their hands. But now a score of warriors advanced warily, bows and arrows ready.

Talker-Between spoke for them—no longer smiling, but full of questions now. Why were the white men still here? Two ships had returned across the great water many moons ago. Why had they stayed?

David saw the captain's jaw tighten. They had sowed a crop of lies in the spring. Nothing for it now but to tell more lies.

So the captain lied. Their third ship, he said, was not seaworthy. Their leader had gone back for help. They awaited his return. They had come to trade for corn. They brought fine copper.

The warriors muttered together, and Talker-Between gave their answer. They had no corn to trade for copper. They would trade for guns and swords.

Again the captain shook his head. No guns and swords to trade; only copper. He held out copper for them to see. Some of the Indians drew near and babbled excitedly, but others shouted angrily and called them back.

In the boat, the white men began to argue, too. Why not trade a few guns now? For just enough food to tide them over until Newport arrived? That was all they needed! If the Indians insisted on guns . . .

"They want copper," John Smith answered. "Remember that! When they find they can't get guns, they will take copper and be glad to get it! When—"

He stopped. The warriors, moving suddenly as one man, fitted arrows into their bows and stepped forward.

"Ready!" the captain ordered. "Aim over their heads! Fire!"

The guns barked. The Indians dropped to the ground and then disappeared into the forest. On board, the men waited. The minutes passed.

"And that," one said bitterly, "is the end of getting corn here!"

"Put in to shore," the captain commanded. He left men to guard the boat; the others, matches lighted and muskets ready, marched to the town of the Kecoughtans.

"Holla!" the captain shouted. Silence. No sign of life. "Keep a sharp lookout," he said. "Don't touch anything."

Warily they advanced toward the bark-covered houses, shoving aside the skin curtains with their muskets, peering into the gloom. Not a living person in the village.

"Ha!" one man laughed. "We scared them off! And here's the corn! We'll load our—"

"Stop!" the captain roared. "We will not steal!"

"But we've got to have corn! If they won't trade for copper—"

"They will trade! Back to the shore! March!" Muttering, the men obeyed.

When they reached the shore the captain commanded, "Spread a blanket. Put copper on it so they can see."

"So *who* can see?"

"The Indians. They're watching us, all right."

They spread the blanket, and put copper on it; they waited. Not an Indian appeared. Again the men muttered.

Suddenly a hideous shout rose from the forest, and a

horde of warriors advanced, yelling, brandishing spears. Two Indians, in front of the others, carried a fiendish-looking idol between them.

A gun barked. One of the Indians carrying the idol clutched his arm. The other dropped the idol and whirled toward his companion.

"Get it!" the captain yelled. Two men dashed forward, grabbed the idol, and dashed back to their companions.

A great cry rose from the Indians now—not a war shout—but a wail. "Okee! Okee!" They fled back into the forest.

John Smith shouted to Talker-Between. The god Okee was safe. The white men would not harm him. They had come to trade. When they had traded, they would give back Okee.

Silence. Again they waited. At last the Indians emerged from the forest, carrying corn. They would trade, they said—for copper.

When the shallop was one-third full, John Smith said, "That is enough. Give them their god, Okee."

The men protested. "But we need more corn than this! We need—"

"Shove off!" the captain roared.

He did not speak again until the shallop was moving up the James.

"I know we need more corn," he growled, "but there is no point in letting the Indians know. We'll trade at other villages." He smiled grimly. "We'll have less trouble from here on up the river. Word will reach the other villages that we are trading with copper and not with guns!"

The muttering stopped. Some of the men even smiled.

"Remember!" And he hammered the words home. "We have what they do not have! Metal! It is precious to them! Always remember that! When we go to an Indian village, we do not go to beg or to steal! We go to trade!"

They traded at three more villages; the shallop rode low in the water. The men were singing as they leaned on the oars and sped toward Jamestown.

Suddenly the singing stopped; they stared, bewildered, toward the *Discovery*, anchored at Jamestown. Men crowded the deck, readying her for the sea. That could mean only one thing. The men of Jamestown were deserting and fleeing to England.

CHAPTER EIGHT

Under Spanish Pay

BEFORE the shallop was moored John Smith sprang from it and leaped aboard the *Discovery*.

Captain Martin did not wait for his question. "But Newport is late. He may have been lost. While we have food for the journey, part of us should take the *Discovery* and go to England. We must let them know our situation. We must let them know we need food!"

"We have food!" John Smith roared. "I've traded for corn down the river, and I'll trade for corn up the river. But we'll not desert Jamestown!"

"We're not deserting!" Captain Archer shouted. "We men on the council have voted to go for help. We have—"

"What are *you* doing on the council?"

President Ratcliffe said, "I nominated him, and the council voted to seat him! We—"

"You have no power to elect or appoint a man to the council!" John Smith declared. "Only the London Company can seat men on the Council of Virginia! Captain Archer cannot be seated, and he can't vote to desert Jamestown."

"We are not deserting!" President Ratcliffe said. "We are going for help. Even without Archer's vote, the vote is four to one against you! Vote against it if you want to, but that is all you can do!"

"Oh, no, it isn't all I can do! Before I'd see this ship leave Virginia, I'd sink her!"

"You wouldn't dare!"

"I dare do anything that keeps you from deserting Jamestown. Well, do I sink her, or don't I?"

After a silence, Captain Martin spoke. "Just what do you mean?"

"Do I have your word that you won't desert Jamestown?"

The men on the shallop held their breath as they waited. Finally the men on the *Discovery* shook hands with John Smith—Martin first, then Ratcliffe, and finally Kendall. Captain Archer stalked away.

Ratcliffe called, "Archer? Do we have your word, too?"

"I don't need his word," John Smith said. "He is not part of the council."

Captain Ratcliffe did not answer that. He came aboard the shallop, inspected the supply of corn, and praised the men. He smiled at John Smith and clapped him on the shoulder. "Excellent! Excellent! Tomorrow, I suggest you go upriver and trade for more."

John Smith nodded. "Now is the time to trade. I'll take the *Discovery* instead of the shallop."

Ratcliffe frowned. "Why so?"

"Why not? She will hold more corn. She's ready to sail. And she isn't going anywhere else just now, is she?"

Ratcliffe flushed, and snapped, "Very well! Take her!"

Three times they went up the James and returned with corn. Three times, as they returned, the men on the *Discovery* craned their necks for sight of Newport's ship. But Newport had not come.

When they returned the third time, Captain Ratcliffe came aboard the *Discovery* and ordered them to put out from shore.

When they were out of hearing of the fort, he said, "There is a plot afoot. I don't know what it is, nor who is involved. None of the men here with you, Captain Smith. Because it has been brewing since you left. Tonight, I'm going to try to unearth the trouble. When I do, I'll need you and these men to stand back of me."

"We'll be ready," John Smith promised.

"I think," Ratcliffe said grimly, "that I know the man I can frighten into talking."

That evening he wheeled suddenly, and grabbed James Read, the blacksmith, by his shirt. "You there! I know you're in the thick of it! Are you going to confess, or do you want to hang?"

The blacksmith glowered and muttered, "I'm not in the thick of anything. And any man that says I am is—"

"Don't lie to me, you—"

With a hoarse growl James Read drew back his huge fist to strike. Instantly four men grabbed him from behind.

Ratcliffe looked pleased. "So," he said, "you were about to strike the president of the Virginia Colony. That's mutiny! Do you know the punishment for mutiny?"

David heard the sharp hiss of indrawn breath. The blacksmith paled.

"I'll be merciful," Ratcliffe went on. "After the trial, I'll ask that you be hanged by your neck until you are dead. I could ask for a harsher sentence, you know. I could ask that you be hanged by your neck until you are half dead, and then be drawn and quartered."

"I wasn't in any plot."

The trial did not take long. James Read, blacksmith, was sentenced to die.

"Do you understand?" Ratcliffe said. "You're going to hang! Who was in the plot with you?"

James Read's eyes were level. "I wasn't in any plot."

Ratcliffe hesitated a moment, then said, "Hang him!"

Men hesitated, too, then grabbed the blacksmith's arms, and shoved him toward the gallows. Halfway there, the bravado went out of James Read.

"I'll tell! I'll tell! It's a plot to betray us to the Spaniards!"

A growl of rage swept through the men around James Read. Captain Kendall's hand flashed to his sword. "Why, that—"

Ratcliffe grabbed Kendall's arm. "No! He'll be executed according to law! Not run through in anger!" Still holding the arm of the fiery captain, he said, "All right, James Read, tell us what you have to tell."

The blacksmith's guard pulled him to his feet. "I was in the plot to betray us to the Spaniards."

"Who was in the plot with you? Tell me," Ratcliffe shouted, "if you want to save your own neck!"

The blacksmith raised his hand. "So help me God, sir, I don't know. I only know the leader. Captain Kendall." He straightened. "And if you think I'm lying, sir, I can tell you where letters from the Spanish are hidden! Letters addressed to Captain Kendall!"

Ratcliffe's hooded eyes stared long and hard at the blacksmith. At last he turned to Kendall. "Well?"

A shrug was Kendall's only answer.

Ratcliffe's eyes narrowed. "You admit you were the leader of the plot?"

Kendall's thin lips twisted. "I am always a leader!"

"Who else was in the plot with you?"

Kendall shrugged again. "Why worry about that? When the leader is dead, you have nothing to worry about." He lifted his chin. "I ask my right as an English-man—to be tried by a jury of my peers. And after the trial, I ask my right as a gentleman—to be shot instead of hanged."

During the trial, Kendall did not lose his haughty air. "After all, I like to be on the winning side. We English-men have proved—very miserably—that we cannot colo-nize. The Spanish have proved—very magnificently—that they can."

"You came on this expedition," Ratcliffe asked, "for the sole purpose of betraying us into Spanish hands?"

Kendall lifted his eyebrows. "Not at all! If we Englishmen had made a success of Jamestown, I'd have betrayed the Spaniards. But what have we done? We've settled one miserable little neck of land, and lost about three-fourths of the expedition in doing it. And—if you are fools enough to stay here—the rest of you will die." He smiled his one-sided smile again. "When I knew that Jamestown was going to fail, I began to choose the men who would go over to the Spanish with me—men who would rather be on the winning side." His smile widened. "I'm an excellent judge of men. Not a single man I talked to has turned me down."

Ratcliffe's hand flashed to his sword. "Who are they?"

"Nothing you can do will make me tell."

When they pronounced the sentence, Kendall did not flinch. When they stood him before the firing squad, he spurned the blindfold and faced his executioners.

One last time Ratcliffe shouted, "Who was in the plot with you? Who?"

Kendall smiled. "That's what you will always be wondering, isn't it?"

The president gave the signal; the guns spoke.

That night men did not gather in little groups to talk; they stood apart, and every man sent a sidelong glance at another. In every man's eyes was the question: Who were the traitors? Who plotted to betray them to the Spaniards? *Who?*

The only man who could answer was dead.

November ended; December came. Still no sign of Newport. Again the men began muttering. Newport was not coming. The thing to do was to leave Jamestown now, while they had food enough for the voyage.

"The thing to do," President Ratcliffe said to Captain Smith, "is to try to find the passage to the China Sea. The Chickahominy River seems to bear more to the north. If you take the shallop up the James and into the Chicka-hominy . . . those Indians have been friendly . . . and explore for the route by that river . . ."

"If I leave the *Discovery* here," John Smith said, "will she be here when I return?"

"She will!" Ratcliffe declared. "I have no intention of deserting Jamestown!"

They shook hands, and John Smith chose his crew. "Emory, Robinson, Casson, Mills, Warren . . ."

Someone named Warren is going, David thought. I wish I could . . . *I'm Warren!* And he saluted and turned away quickly before anyone should see him blush with pleasure. Confound it! He'd grown like a weed this last year. Why didn't he stop blushing like a girl?

A brisk breeze carried them up the river, past once-green marshes that had turned brown, then white, as the tide water spangled them with salt crystals. Between the evergreens of the forest David saw holly trees, laden with red berries.

Deck the hall with boughs of holly . . .

Was it only a year ago that he had left his warm bed in England, and tramped through the snow with Jem, to find holly? Only a year since Jem had been singing . . . His throat ached and he swallowed hard. He was glad when the wind died and they had to break out the oars. Anything was better than remembering.

That night a few straggling wild geese flew over, with their haunting cry. Night came, and a sudden fog swallowed the world. They felt their way ashore. In the morning, the sun turned the fog into a golden mist. They stayed at anchor until the brown leaves stopped drifting downriver, whirled about slowly, and began to move up the river.

With the rising tide they weighed anchor, and moved north into the Chickahominy. *A river bearing north and west.* Was this the river that would lead them to the divide? Could they follow this river to its head, then portage across to a river flowing west, into the China Sea?

"If we find the route to the China Sea," one said . . .

And the shallop stopped. A sand bar. They managed to rock the boat off.

"There may be deeper water ahead," their captain said.

He went ashore to an Indian village and bargained for a canoe and two guides.

"Robinson and Emory, you'll come with me. You others anchor the shallop well out from shore and stay with it."

"We may go ashore to hunt a bit," George Casson said. "But if we do, we'll not lose sight of—"

"You'll stay with the shallop!" John Smith ordered. "Is that understood?"

"Yes, Captain Smith!"

But when the canoe had disappeared up the river, the men began muttering.

"He saw something ashore that he's keeping to himself."

"Gold-showing ore, most likely."

"I say we have as much right ashore as he does!"

"I say so, too!"

They quarreled briefly about who would remain in the shallop. Finally they cast lots. Mills was the unlucky fellow who had to stay in the shallop with David. When the others had gone ashore, Mills and David rowed back out into the river and anchored. The men disappeared into the forest. For a time they could hear the crackling of twigs, the sound of their voices. Then silence.

The minutes dragged. David's teeth chattered.

Mills growled, "I say we go ashore and build a fire to get warm."

"My orders," David said, "were to stay with the shallop! That's what I'm doing!"

Mills was almost as big as Jem had been. Now his dark eyes mocked. "What a little man!" he sneered. "Stay if you want to, but I—"

Suddenly a bloodcurdling howl rose from the forest.

"Get down!" Mills shouted, and threw himself flat in the shallop.

But David sat, numb with shock. The yells rose to an echoing din. The crew of the shallop dashed from the forest, splashed into the water, flung themselves into the boat. George Casson was last, running with outflung arms, gasping. Just as he reached the riverbank, an arrow hissed from the forest and struck him. He jerked, sprawled, and lay, face down, in the water.

The men in the shallop grabbed the oars. The shallop jerked and swerved around on her cable.

"Cut it!" one yelled. "Cut it!"

One slashed at the cable. The shallop spurted across the river and then downstream, beyond range of the arrows.

David came out of his shock. "The captain!"

"Dead," one said, "or he will be. No chance to reach him."

"We can't desert him! We can't—" David leaped for the stern of the boat. Something exploded against his head.

When he opened his eyes, the shallop was under sail, moving down the James.

Mills bent over him. "Coming around, are you?"

"What hit me?"

"I did. If I hadn't, you'd have jumped in the river. I guess you had some crazy notion of reaching the captain."

"But we can't just—"

Mills sighed with weary patience. "Look, lad, there wasn't a chance of saving him. Our men landed right in the middle of an Indian hunt."

All the men tried to explain.

"Hundreds of Indians!"

"A good hundred, at least, between us and the captain!"

"There wasn't a chance to reach him!"

"The thing for us to do is to get back to Jamestown with the word!"

"That's right! President Ratcliffe has to know who is dead! Casson, Robinson, Emory, and John Smith."

"No point in the rest of us getting killed, was there?"

David could not answer. He sat with chattering teeth, staring miserably into the water.

"Just shock," Mills said. "We shouldn't have brought a younker with us. Too young to stomach it."

CHAPTER NINE

"To Overcome Is to Live"

BACK at the fort, the crew of the shallop faced the shocked eyes of George Percy and Master Hunt, the anger of President Ratcliffe, and tried to explain.

Yes, they had disobeyed orders when they had gone ashore. Yes, they had angered the Indians by plunging into the middle of their hunting circle. Yes, they had fled. No, they had not tried to reach the captain.

"How could we?" they said. "The river was too shallow for our boat. He had the canoe. We didn't."

Then they began to ask questions, too, and the news of Jamestown was just as grim. No, there was no word of Newport yet. Newport, who was a month overdue!

The handful of survivors on James Island looked at each other. More than a hundred men when Newport sailed in June; only thirty-seven alive now.

Captain Archer began to talk. It was no use hoping for help from England! The only thing to do was to abandon the colony. They'd take what food they had, and sail to the West Indies. At least they would be warm. They could winter there, then lay in stores and sail for home.

Half the men agreed with him. But Captain Martin, sick as he was—he had never recovered from the swamp fever—protested. "It was one thing for part of us to try to reach England for help! I was in favor of that. But to give up Jamestown? No!"

"Stay if you want to!" Archer shouted. "But any of us who have good sense are leaving! If we of the council—"

Ratcliffe smiled. "You have only one vote. The rest of the council . . ." He stopped and stared, wordless, at Captain Martin.

And the men of Jamestown stared, too. Not counting Archer, there were only two men of the council now. Five seats were vacant: Wingfield—accused of hoarding food and deposed; Kendall—convicted of treachery and executed; Gosnold—dead; Newport—lost at sea; Smith—no chance that he was not dead, too.

Ratcliffe's smile faded. "The decision," he said grimly, "rests with the council. You favor going; Captain Martin favors staying." His smile flicked again. "The decision really depends on me, doesn't it? I have two votes."

Again the men of Jamestown gathered in muttering groups. Only when Master Hunt called them to evening prayer was the grumbling silent. He prayed for the safety of Captain Newport and his crew; he prayed for Captain Smith and his two companions. He pronounced the benediction:

"Arise, and go in peace and may the peace of God go with you."

The men rose and scattered, to gather again in grumbling huddles.

Captain Archer and three others climbed to one of the bulwarks of the fort to examine the demi-culverin.

Ratcliffe and Martin watched. Ratcliffe smiled. "Suppose they think they could mount that cannon on the *Discovery?* Be amusing to watch them try, wouldn't it? Try to mount one on deck, and you'd overset her—just like that!" He snapped his fingers.

Captain Archer and his companions must have come to the same conclusion; they shrugged, climbed down from the bulwark, and strolled away.

For three days Archer strode about, talking to one man and then another. For three days President Ratcliffe mounted lookouts on the bulwarks to watch for the return of Newport. The third evening he shrugged in surrender and joined the group around Archer.

Heartsick, David watched. They were going to abandon Jamestown. All night he stared into the dark and hunted for some solution, but there was none. If Ratcliffe decided to give up, that settled it.

When dawn sent slivers of light between the planks of his thatched cabin, David rose, shivering, pulled on his coat and shoes, and opened the door. Already men crowded the deck of the *Discovery,* checking her sails and rigging. David climbed to a bulwark and stared bitterly toward the forest on the mainland. Not even a year, and they were giving up. Maybe Kendall was right when he said that Englishmen could not colonize. Over a hundred years since the first English sailed with Cabot, and what had they done? They had named a part of the American coast Virginia. Sir Walter Raleigh had brought back two plants from the new world. He had grown white potatoes on his Irish estate; he had taught men to smoke tobacco. A vegetable and a weed—that was all the English had to show for a hundred years of trying. And now they were giving up again. They—

He stiffened. A shadow moved in the forest. As he watched, two Indians emerged and approached the neck of land to James Island. One carried a paper. They reached the gate, dropped the paper, turned, and fled back to the forest.

David fumbled to open the heavy gate and grabbed the paper. One glance at the slashing scrawl and his tiredness fell away. John Smith was alive! Waving the letter, he dashed to the pinnace. "He's alive! He's alive!"

Ratcliffe snatched the letter, opened it, and read. His hooded eyes raced back and forth over the lines; his scowl did not relax. The men who gathered about him did not smile. They only waited. "From Captain Smith," he said. "He's a captive of the great Powhatan."

"What about Robinson and Emory?" Archer asked.

"Dead."

"And John Smith is a captive of the great Powhatan? What does he expect us to do?"

Ratcliffe began to read:

"So far, I have staved off my execution by making the Indians believe I have Great Medicine. When the men who brought this letter return with the gifts I have asked for here, Powhatan will be convinced that I have Great Medicine. Be sure to send another compass. I surrendered my own in a good cause. Explain that the compass will lead them back to me. I am almost due north of James Island, on the north bank of the next great river—the Pamunkey.

"If you fail me, I shall die; if you follow my directions, I hope to cement a friendship with the great Powhatan that will stand us in good stead.

"Do not show fear or concern. Treat the messengers well, but impress them with our power. Fire one of the cannon. Have Amos Todkill—he is a master marksman—shoot at a difficult mark.

"Remember! Send everything I have asked for, smile on the messengers, and scare them within an inch of their lives!"

When Ratcliffe finished reading, some of the men stamped and cheered. Others shot lowering glances at each other.

Archer stared at the letter with narrowed eyes. "If he is still alive, there is only one explanation. He has made a deal with Powhatan."

"Nothing of the sort!" George Percy said. "He's using his wits to stay alive and to help the colony! To—"

Others shouted him down.

"He's using his wits to save himself!"

"Yes! He sent those Indians to get a look at the fort!"

"Right! So they will know how to attack us!"

"He'll probably lead the charge against us, himself!"

"I say—kill the messengers!"

"That's it! And sail while Powhatan is still waiting for them to return!"

Master Hunt began to plead, but they shouted him down, too. One ran to summon the messengers into the fort.

David did not know just what he meant to do, but he did not stop until he had left the fort, crossed the neck of land, and was in the forest, armed with a pistol and a compass. Hidden there, he waited, watching the fort. If the messengers did not leave the fort alive . . .

After an hour, he saw the two Indians coming. One carried a bundle; the other walked, head bent, intent on a compass in his outstretched hand.

David stepped from his place of hiding, called to them, and held out his compass. They stopped short, staring at him. Slowly, they came nearer. They paused again. He laid his hand on his heart. He pointed to his compass again, then to the north.

Motionless, the Indians stared at him.

I might as well pretend everything is all right, he told himself. Tapping his compass, he smiled, turned, faced north, and began walking. No sound behind him. Not a twig snapped. His heart hammered until the blood beat in his ears. He fought the impulse to look back, to run, to dart behind a tree.

When the Indians had come from the forest, they had carried no arms. But had they hidden their bows and arrows? Were they picking up their bows now? Were they fitting an arrow, and taking aim? He thought of the day on the Chickahominy, and George Casson fleeing toward the riverbank. He remembered the hiss of the arrow that struck him—how Casson stopped, stiffened, then sprawled, arms outflung, and lay face down in the river.

Out of the tail of his eye he saw a shadow. He flinched and fought to smother a gasp, for the Indians were with him, one on either side, stalking through the forest without a sound. He forced himself to smile; he wondered if they could hear the way his heart was hammering.

At the Pamunkey River they brought a canoe out of hiding, and ferried him across to the north bank, and to the village of the great Powhatan. Still without talking they led the way past rows of tunnel-like huts to a hut on the northern edge of the village. They stopped before the skin-covered doorway and called a greeting.

When from within the hut John Smith's voice called an answer, David's knees began to shake. His hands were shaking, too. He stared hard at the bark-covered hut, but it swam in front of his eyes. The sleepless night, the strain of the journey . . . but even while he shook he could feel his grin spreading.

John Smith flung back the curtain of skin. He gave no sign that he saw David. He listened while the Indians talked; he answered them in their own tongue. They went away. Not until they were out of earshot did he stare at David. "What are you doing here?"

"S-s-s-sir?" David shut his eyes and shook his head to fight off the dizziness, the swimming fog around him.

"Get inside," the captain barked, "if you can't stand up!"

David lurched into the hut, choked on the smoke, stumbled, and sat down on a pallet of skins.

John Smith followed him inside. "Well! Answer me! What are you doing here?"

David clenched his teeth and waited until he was sure his voice was steady. "I came because you are needed at Jamestown. The men are ready to desert. They were overhauling the pinnace when your message came."

"Newport has not come?"

"No, sir. And they need you. I thought if the Indians had me for a hostage, they might let you go."

"You thought Powhatan would take you in my place? And be satisfied with the bargain?"

"I—I—guess I hadn't thought of that, sir."

"You hadn't thought." The captain sat down on the other pallet of skins. "What happened on the Chickahominy? What has been happening since?"

David told him everything, down to the plan to abandon Jamestown. "At first, Captain Ratcliffe didn't give up. It was Archer who was the traitor!"

John Smith sighed and rubbed his hand over his forehead. "No . . . not a traitor. . . . He had just reached his breaking point. But Ratcliffe was determined to hold on?"

"Until yesterday, sir. Then he gave up, too. If your letter had not come when it did—and even then I wasn't sure they would send the messengers back. They were talking about killing them. So I—I ran away. And I brought you this gun."

"So I see." The captain took the gun, opened it, and removed part of the mechanism. "I did that to my gun, too."

"But—but—"

"Guns won't do us any good. So the only thing is to see that they won't do the Indians any good either." He almost smiled. "Two of Powhatan's warriors have been trying for three days to fire my gun. And they have taken my pouch of powder. They are saving it to plant next spring."

"Planting powder!" David laughed softly, and his laugh grew louder.

"*Stop it!*" When David was silent, the captain stared at him for a long moment. "You hare-brained, headlong, idiotic, half-witted . . ." He smiled suddenly. "You know, we may get out of this alive, yet! If that fellow I wounded gets well . . ."

"What happened to the three of you?" David asked. "You and Robinson and Emory?"

"When we couldn't take the canoe further, I left Robinson and Emory there, with one guide, and went ahead on foot with the other. When I heard the Indians yell, I grabbed my guide and strapped him to my arm—sort of a buckler. The Indians attacked. I fired once, and wounded one of them. That slowed them down for a moment. I might have got away, but I was walking backward—couldn't see where I was going. I stepped into a bog, and sank up to my waist. They captured me."

"Robinson and Emory?"

"They killed them."

"But they didn't kill you . . ." David said.

The captain shrugged. "I made them believe I had Great Medicine. The compass helped. We were traveling north. It puzzled them that the needle pointed our way. Even here in the village, the compass puzzles them. My hut is on the northern edge, you see, and the needle is still pointing toward me. So they still think I have Great Medicine. They are afraid if they kill me that the wounded man will die. So . . . if he gets well . . ."

"What if he dies?" David asked.

"That's why I said you were a fool to come! We've got to get you out of here and back to Jamestown." The captain jumped to his feet and paced the length of the narrow, smoky house. "We'll think of something. Meantime, keep your head up. Impress them. No matter what happens, do not show fear. If they decide to do away with me, don't try anything foolish. Just watch your chance to escape."

"But if I—"

"That's an order!"

"Yes, sir."

The captain spoke more quietly. "This is a battle of wits, David, so keep your wits about you."

"Yes, sir."

"And learn everything you can. You may have a chance to pick up quite a few Indian words."

"How long do you think . . ."

"I haven't the slightest idea. Come, let's walk about the village."

They watched the Indians making a canoe of a huge log. They had hollowed it out about six inches deep, and small fires were burning the length of the shallow trough. As David watched, the Indians swept the fire to one end of the trough, and scraped at the charred wood with shells.

"Is that the way they will hollow out the whole log?"

The captain nodded. "A very tedious business. They've nothing to work with but flint, fire, and shells. That's why our metal is valuable to them. So long as we never trade weapons for corn, they will always be glad to get metal. Always remember that, David!"

"Yes, sir."

The days crawled by. The Indians gave them the run of the village. They fed them well.

"You'd think," John Smith remarked one night at supper, "that they were cannibals, and fattening me up for a state occasion." He yawned, stretched on his pallet, and slept.

The day before Christmas, when David wakened, he was alone in the hut. Had the Indians? . . . He jumped to his feet, dashed to the doorway, jerked the skin curtain aside, then stopped just in time. *No matter what happens, do not show fear.* He must remember that.

An Indian brought him breakfast. When he had eaten, he strolled about the village, trying to stalk as proudly and to frown as sternly as the captain. He went to all the places where he thought John Smith might be, but there was no sign of him. David knew he could not ask questions; he could only wait. Late in the afternoon he went back to the hut and stretched out on his bed of skins. That close to the ground, the smoke did not sting his eyes so much.

Christmas Eve . . . just a year ago. . . .

He remembered his last day at home, floundering through the snow behind Jem, trying to match his stride. If Jem were here now . . . He swallowed hard and squeezed his eyelids tight against the tears. Then he heard, or thought he heard, singing:

> "Deck the hall with boughs of holly!
> Fa la la la la la la la la!
> 'Tis the season to be jolly!
> Fa la la la la la la la la!"

Was he dreaming, or had he lost his mind? He ran to the door, thrust aside the skin curtain, and came face to face with John Smith and two Indians, laden with stacks of holly.

John Smith stopped singing for one moment to mutter, "*You squaw!*" His hand, with fingers widespread, caught David in the chest and flung him backward into the hut.

Outside, the song began again, and moved around the hut. They must be decorating it with the holly.

When David's anger cooled, he realized he was crouched on one knee, with a stone in his hand. He took a deep breath, let it out slowly, and laid down the rock. When John Smith entered, David waited for him to speak, but the captain said nothing.

Finally David broke the silence. "Thank you for—getting me out of sight. I—I—was thinking about Jem and —I'm all right if I don't hear Christmas songs."

"You'll hear them tonight," the captain said. "I've told the Indians that this is a great feast night when we sing to the White Man's God."

At dusk, when the Indians brought food, another followed with a drum, made of a hollowed-out piece of log, covered with skin; he set it down and laid two round-headed drumsticks on it.

John Smith grinned. "I asked for the drum. If we can start the Indians keeping time to our songs, they'll believe more than ever in my Great Medicine."

David remembered last Christmas Eve in the Thames—three shiploads of men, shouting "Wassail" and stamping. He grinned, too. He felt better now.

I can bear anything, he told himself, but "The Coventry Carol," and we won't be singing that. It's no sort of song to beat time to on a drum.

That night he sat in the smoky hut, shouting the songs, taking his turn at beating time on the drum. "Deck the Hall"—"God Rest You Merry, Gentlemen"—"Wassail." They sang them all three times.

The captain laid down the drumsticks, stretched, and yawned. "I don't know 'The Coventry Carol.' You'll have to sing that alone."

"No, please, Captain Smith, I'll—"

"What's the matter? Aren't you man enough? Sing it through twice!" He stretched on his bed, and linked his fingers behind his head. "Keep singing it until I tell you to stop."

For a moment David's rage was thick in his throat and hot on his face. Then he was cold. *You'll eat those words!* he thought. *Some day you'll eat those words!* Softly, steadily, he began to sing:

"Lul-lay, Thou little tiny Child!
By, by, lully, lul-lay . . ."

117

When he had finished, his anger was gone. He sang it again; he even held the last note, letting it swell and fade as Jem had sung it.

The captain stirred, stretched, and sat up. "Thank you, David. It's good to know I have a man I can depend on."

"A . . . man?"

"Manhood isn't a matter of inches or years. It's a matter of overcoming childhood. When you sang that song, you overcame the child you were a year ago. That is good. To overcome is to live."

"Thank you."

"You're going to need to be a man. I have orders for you."

"Yes, Captain?"

"Tomorrow, you'll watch your chance, and go back to Jamestown."

"You mean . . ."

"The man I wounded isn't going to get well. The mark of death is on his face."

"Oh . . ."

The captain gripped David's hand. "It must be midnight. Merry Christmas, David. Time we went to sleep. Get plenty of rest. You'll need it tomorrow."

In two minutes the captain's light, even breathing said he slept. David stretched on his bed of skins, closed his eyes, and tried to sleep, too. But too many things had happened too fast; the toughest, sternest, harshest man he had ever known had called him "a man to depend on." Tomorrow, he must desert that man and try to reach Jamestown. How would he get across the river? Could he swim the icy water, and then reach Jamestown before he froze to death?

Before dawn an eerie, wailing cry wakened him. He sat up, dazed, as four Indians, shouting angrily, crowded into the hut.

John Smith stood and waited, motionless. When two of them grabbed his arms, he made no resistance. Instead, he began to sing with a punchy, insistent rhythm. The tune was "Deck the Hall," but the words were strange:

> "You can't save me, so don't try to!
> Fa la la la la la la la la!
> You can't save me, so don't try to!
> Fa la la la la la la la la!"

He was still singing when his captors shoved him through the doorway.

CHAPTER TEN

"Yet No Man Remembered . . ."

THE other two Indians grabbed David's arms, jerked him to his feet, and dragged him from the hut.

Dawn was an ominous red that matched the huge camp-fire as they walked to the center of the village. The great Powhatan sat on a high, bedlike throne, covered with skins. Behind him towered painted warriors. On either side of him, at his feet, sat women and children.

In front of the throne a warrior stood with one foot resting on a huge rock. In his hands he held a heavy, knotted club, the thickest part as big as his leg.

The captain stopped singing, but his stride did not falter. David heard the cadence of the words he murmured; it was a prayer of confession. A deafening shout of triumph rose from the Indians. John Smith knelt by the rock.

Unconsciously, David tried to turn away, but his captors jerked his elbows behind him and thrust him forward where—unless he closed his eyes—he would be forced to watch the executioner's club come down. He swallowed, fighting nausea, and stared straight ahead, keeping his gaze focused on a spot beyond the captain's body.

Powhatan stood and began to speak. His voice rose and fell in thundering, majestic cadences. On and on. . . . Would he never stop talking? At last he gave a gesture of command. John Smith bowed his head against the rock. The executioner lifted his club and whirled it about his head.

Another deafening shout rose, then broke suddenly. Silence. David saw a blur of white. A girl had dashed to the rock, and was holding John Smith's head in her arms. It was Pocahontas, one of Powhatan's daughters.

With grunts of amazement David's captors released him. He swayed and staggered to get his balance. Don't faint! he told himself. If you do, John Smith will give you the devil! He stared hard at the branch of a tree until it stopped swimming. Dimly at first, then more clearly, he heard Powhatan's stern questions and the girl's soft answers.

Suddenly the mighty Powhatan laughed, nodded, and gave a careless command. The executioner turned away. John Smith stood, shrugged to settle his doublet, and bowed over the girl's hand.

She smiled shyly, and, taking the captain's hand, led
him toward Powhatan. Again Powhatan talked in majestic
cadences. John Smith was motionless, his eyes on the chieftain's face. Pocahontas was motionless, too, her eyes on
the captain.

At last Powhatan stopped talking, stretched out his

hand, and seemed to be pronouncing a blessing over the man he had ordered to be put to death. Another shout arose that sounded as threatening as the earlier ones. But Pocahontas still smiled and held John Smith's hand.

David's captors led him back to his hut. One guarded him; another brought him food. When he had eaten, he walked to the door. An Indian stood outside, on guard. David went back and stretched on his bed.

It was midmorning when the captain came to the hut, still walking hand in hand with Pocahontas. "I've been adopted," he said. "It seems to be a custom. If a favored child asks for a captive, she may have him."

"Will they let you go back to Jamestown?"

John Smith's eyes twinkled. "They can't see any reason why I should want to go back, but sooner or later I'll persuade them. Meantime, they have agreed to send you back. They are waiting now, to take you across the river."

David hesitated. "You—you're sure I can't—"

"You have your orders! Get back to Jamestown!" John Smith barked. Then, more quietly, he said, "Tell them I'm alive, that I'm on friendly terms with Powhatan, and that I'll be back soon."

"Yes, sir."

Two Indians ferried him across the Pamunkey, pointed the way, and left him on the south bank. When David neared James Island, he climbed a tree and looked for sight of Newport's ship. But only the *Discovery* rode at anchor. So Newport had not returned. Well . . . at least they had not deserted Jamestown.

When the watchman opened the gate, David hurried to President Ratcliffe, smiling, telling him the good news.

The men crowded round him. Master Hunt and George Percy shook his hand. Some of the soldiers slapped him on the back. But most of the survivors of Jamestown stared at him coldly.

"What happened?" Ratcliffe asked.

When David had finished, Captain Archer sneered. "I've heard some of John Smith's tales, but that is the prize lie of them all! And *you*—" He leveled a finger at David. "You should be put in irons for leaving the fort without permission!"

"But when I went, sir," David said, "I thought everyone was leaving Jamestown. I didn't want to desert the colony, so—"

Captain Archer flushed. "Are you calling me a deserter?"

"No, sir. I guess you just reached your—your breaking point."

"*What!*"

"That's what Captain Smith said. That you are not really traitors; you've just reached your breaking point. That's why you want to give up." He straightened. "Well, I haven't reached my breaking point yet! So if I abandoned Jamestown, I'd feel like a deserter!"

Archer's eyes blazed. "We are not deserters! It's only common sense to abandon Jamestown. It's six months since Newport sailed! Can't you see there is no hope of his returning?"

"The first colony of Roanoke gave up," David said. "If they had held on two weeks longer—"

"Another word out of you, and you'll sit in the stocks with a gag in your mouth!" Archer roared, and he walked away with President Ratcliffe.

Master Hunt looked after them, his eyes troubled. "I thank God, David, that you dared to go to Powhatan's village. And I thank God that you got back when you did. Another day, and you would have found the fort empty—Jamestown deserted."

"They'll not give up now, will they?"

The minister sighed. "I wish I knew. Perhaps . . . if it is not too long . . ."

But the year ended, and the new year began. No word from John Smith; no sign of Captain Newport. The sixth of January they wooded and watered the *Discovery*. The morning of the seventh, Captain Ratcliffe ordered everyone on board for a meeting.

When everyone was on the pinnace, he said, "Weigh anchor!"

A babel of protests, questions, cheers, and more questions arose.

"The cannon! We're leaving the cannon!"

"The *Discovery* cannot handle their weight."

"The food in the storehouse? We can't go without—"

Ratcliffe smiled. "Everything was stowed aboard last night. I'm done with arguments. Topmen into the rigging!" He looked at David. "Lay aloft!"

"I won't go! I won't go!"

Ratcliffe's smile faded. "David Warren, as president

of the Council of Virginia, I order you to go. If you do not go, that is mutiny. Dealing with mutiny will cause a slight delay—but very slight. Do I make myself clear?"

From the bow a man shouted, "Anchor's a-peak!"

"Then break her out!" Ratcliffe commanded. "Lay aloft topmen!"

From shore a voice bellowed, "Belay! Or I'll sink the ship!"

On the deck of the pinnace men wheeled, stared, and saw John Smith on the nearest bulwark of the fort, with a cannon trained on the hull of the *Discovery*. A handful of men cheered; they shoved and pushed to be first to leave the ship.

"Clear the ship!" he bellowed again, "or I'll sink her!"

"That's murder!" Ratcliffe shouted.

John Smith laughed. "Oh, no! You won't die! You'll jump for shore fast enough when she starts to sink!"

Slowly the last of the men filed off the pinnace. John Smith came down from the bulwark, and was surrounded by a few who cheered. Ratcliffe, Archer, and most of the others stood in a huddle, watching.

"First," Captain Smith said, "we must take care of my guides." He nodded toward three Indians, waiting motionless by the gate. "I promised Powhatan I would send him presents."

Archer took a threatening step forward. "And what did you promise him?"

"A grindstone and two guns."

A babble of anger began. Archer's shout was loudest. "So! When we were starving, you threatened our lives if we traded guns! But now, when it is a matter of saving your own neck, you have changed your song!"

John Smith smiled. "A grindstone and two guns. And I am a man of my word." He led the Indians to the grindstone—a wheel eight inches thick, and almost a yard across.

The Indians pulled, tugged, and wrestled with the grindstone, and finally gave up.

"No?" John Smith sounded regretful. "Too bad. But you shall have the guns." He pointed to the demi-culverins, mounted on the bulwark facing the shore. "Yours! All yours!"

The Indians climbed to the bulwark, to tug at the cannon. They climbed down again, jabbering reproaches.

Captain Smith nodded to Amos Todkill. "Load it with chain shot, and aim at a tree."

When the cannon roared, the Indians stiffened, clutched each other, and stared. They saw the whirling chain shot strike a tree and bring a great limb crashing to the ground. They turned to the captain, bowed their heads, and spoke in awed tones.

He smiled, gave them trinkets and copper, and walked with them to the gate. They paused, their hands on their hearts, for another long harangue of farewell. Then, with one last wary look toward the cannon, they hurried off.

John Smith was grinning broadly when he turned back. "Well, I kept my promise. I offered the gifts, didn't I?" A handful of men chuckled. But Ratcliffe and Archer did not smile.

"John Smith," Archer said, "we accuse you of murder!"

For a moment the captain's face was blank. "You," Archer declared, "are responsible for the deaths of Robinson and Emory! They were obeying your command when they left the protection of the shallop and went ahead with you in the canoe! You are guilty, and you will hang for the deaths of those two men!"

Master Hunt gasped. "No, no! You cannot sentence him to death for—"

"I can! I know my law!"

George Percy tried to laugh it off. "Oh, come now, Archer! Just because John Smith stopped the sailing of the pinnace—"

"That has nothing to do with it!" Archer shouted angrily. "I'm talking of his guilt in the deaths of two men! And I say he dies!"

George Percy sobered. "You aren't serious!"

"I am!"

"But you can't sentence him! Only the council can—"

Ratcliffe's hooded eyes were cold. "The council does sentence him. He will hang in the morning."

All that morning and half the afternoon, George Percy and Master Hunt argued and pleaded. The soldiers pleaded, too. But it was no use. The council had spoken.

For the second time David saw John Smith led aboard the *Discovery* in chains. This time, he knew there was no hope.

When the company assembled for evening prayer, Master Hunt stared at them with stricken eyes and read the service in a husky voice. Time came for the benediction. He lifted his hand, then dropped it.

"In two verses of the ninth chapter of Ecclesiastes," he said, "there is a story." Slowly he repeated:

"There was a little city, and a few men within it; and there came a great King against it, and besieged it, and built great bulwarks against it:

"Now there was found in it a poor wise man, and he by his wisdom delivered the city; yet no man remembered that same poor man."

He paused to search the faces before him. He lifted his hand once more for the benediction. His lips moved, but the words were barely audible.

The men rose, and broke into two groups—some around George Percy and Master Hunt—most of them around Ratcliffe and Archer.

"Isn't there anything you can do?" George Percy begged.

Master Hunt bowed his head on his clasped hands. "I cannot move them! It is as though I talked to stones! Only God can save him now!"

CHAPTER ELEVEN

"Fire!"

FROM the bulwark a watchman cried, "Sail ho-o-o-o!" The men of Jamestown shoved and scrambled to be first at the south gate.

"Man the shallop!" Ratcliffe ordered. "I'll go to meet her!"

David was first in the boat. George Percy started forward, but Ratcliffe waved him back. "No! Not you! Only the council! Martin—Archer—come with me!"

With six men at the oars, and three passengers, the shallop sped toward the ship.

"It's Newport!" Captain Archer shouted. And a yell went up from the shallop.

When a ladder dangled from the waist of the ship, David helped steady it while the three men climbed. Then he scrambled up after them. The crew of the shallop yelled protests, but their shouts were drowned in the confusion on board the ship. David lost himself in the confusion and worked his way forward.

Old Tim was there, to grab his hand. "Davy, lad! You've grown a foot!"

"Almost."

"But you're thin—way too thin."

"A little," David admitted. "Sometimes we didn't have much food. Man, are we glad to see you! We thought you were in the bottom of the ocean!"

"We thought we were going to be." Tim's eyes searched the river ahead. "Where is the *Phoenix?* Exploring?"

"The *Phoenix?*"

"The ship that sailed with us when . . . Oh. . . . So she never got here? May God have mercy on their souls."

The first mate shouted commands. The ship got under way. Tim turned to his work. David edged aft, toward the quarter-deck, in time to hear Captain Newport say, "If the *Phoenix* isn't here yet, there is no hope for Captain Nelson. We weren't more than two days from the Chesapeake when the storm struck us." He looked about. "Where is the rest of the council?"

President Ratcliffe reported. Wingfield deposed; Kendall executed; Gosnold dead of swamp fever . . .

"And John Smith? Where is he?"

Archer answered before Ratcliffe could open his mouth. "Sentenced to die in the morning! For his guilt in the deaths of two men!" And he started to tell the story of the attack on the Chickahominy.

He's lying! David thought. He's making it sound the way he wants! That's why they didn't let George Percy come with them to meet the ship! By the time Captain Newport lands, he will believe Archer! He will . . .

But Captain Newport interrupted Archer's story. "I heard about that attack, from the Kecoughtan Indians," he said. "That the men in the shallop went ashore, and landed in the middle of an Indian hunt. Did the men go ashore by John Smith's orders?"

"No, but Robinson and Emory went with him at his orders. They left the protection of the shallop, and—"

Again Newport interrupted. "How many men did you lose besides Gosnold? And those two?"

"There are thirty-eight of us still alive," Ratcliffe said.

Newport stared, speechless. At last he said, "Thirty-eight? Of a hundred and five? But—but—the Kecough-tans said there had been no more Indian attacks! They said John Smith had traded for corn from the mouth of the James to the falls! They said—"

"They died in the summer, before the corn was ripe," Captain Martin said. "They died of starvation and swamp fever."

Newport was still dazed. "Thirty-eight men . . ."

They had reached James Island and were warping the ship to her mooring. Newport glanced at the *Discovery* and his eyes narrowed.

"Why is she ready to sail?"

Ratcliffe stammered, "We were . . . after all . . . it has been six months . . . more than six months since you sailed. You said . . ."

Newport looked down on the handful of men and the handful of cabins that were all that was left of Jamestown. He looked at the settlers crowding the deck of the *Frances and John*, and spoke to his first mate. "It looks as though our settlers will be living on board for a time. They will remain aboard now, until I give permission for them to land."

He turned his back on their protests, and summoned two men. "Mr. Scrivener, Captain Wynne, you will come with me."

The six men went ashore and David followed. Captain Newport introduced the two new members of the council. Matthew Scrivener's firm mouth and kindly eyes reminded David of Captain Gosnold. Captain Wynne was wiry, quick-spoken, with alert, darting glances that seemed to be taking in everything.

Captain Newport stared grimly about him. The silence seemed endless. Then he looked at President Ratcliffe. "Thirty-eight survivors, and you can spare one man for hanging."

Ratcliffe flushed. "It's not my fault they died! The swamp fever and starvation did it! If the Indians had not brought us food in September, there wouldn't be a man alive."

George Percy spoke quickly. "And what did we trade for food?"

Ratcliffe stiffened. "Copper, of course!"

"But what did they want?" George Percy's usually gentle voice was sharp. "What did the Indians want? Guns! And who made us trade for copper? John Smith!

And when we went down the river to the Kecoughtans, who managed to trade for copper with them? John Smith!" He turned to Captain Newport. "Sir, if John Smith had not been a prisoner of Powhatan, that pinnace would not be ready for the sea! When he got back to Jamestown, we were weighing anchor! If he hadn't threatened to hull the ship, we should have sailed! And that is at the bottom of this trumped-up charge against him!"

Ratcliffe, Martin, and Archer all started talking at once.

"Silence!" Newport roared. "Have you done nothing in Jamestown but quarrel? Bring John Smith here!" They brought John Smith from the pinnace. Newport wrung his hand, and introduced the new members of the council. "With Mr. Scrivener and Captain Wynne," he said, "we have six members on the council and seven votes. How many votes are in favor of the execution of John Smith?"

Archer said, "I still claim that he's guilty of—"

"You are not a member of the council!" Newport snapped.

"But I have been—"

"The council is appointed in London! No man here has the right to appoint another member! We have six members and seven votes! How many votes to execute John Smith?"

Not a hand was raised.

"Then suppose we stop bickering and get to work!" Newport said. "I have one hundred and thirty new settlers aboard the *Frances and John*. They came here expecting to find houses ready to welcome them. Here it is—winter —and not enough houses to shelter four dozen men! We have work to do! *Work!*" Again he looked about and shook his head. "I'll not enjoy taking this report back to London. They did not think much of our 'taste of clap-board.' Not much of a return for the thousands of pounds they have invested."

"But what of the gold?" Captain Archer asked.

"Oh, yes . . . the gold." Newport's face became even more grim. As he talked, the scene lived before their eyes.

Late in July he had put in to Plymouth, and had sent a letter ahead of him to London, telling about the barrel of gold-showing earth he had aboard.

"I warned them to keep the matter secret until we had the ore assayed, but you know how those things go."

The men of Jamestown nodded; they knew how rumors could spread:

"I know I can depend on you to say nothing, but we think they have discovered gold in Virginia!"

Then the story would begin to grow:

"I know you won't say anything, but they have discovered gold in Virginia!"

"Gold in Virginia! They brought back a barrel of ore!"

"Gold in Virginia! They brought back a barrel of it! A solid barrel of pure gold!"

"Richer deposits than the gold mines of Peru!"

"Gold in Virginia! The day will come when we'll ballast our ships with gold!"

"Did you heard about Newport? He's back from Virginia—with his ships ballasted with gold!"

Newport smiled wryly. "By the time I reached London, rumor had done its work. Then we got the assayer's report on the barrel of gold-showing earth. Just iron pyrites. The same mineral that had fooled Frobisher. You can imagine the reaction."

Yes, they could imagine:

"Fool's gold!"

"Did you hear about the fools in Virginia? Sending back a barrel of iron pyrites?"

"Of course! I always said if there was gold in Virginia the Spaniards would have found it!"

"Gold in Virginia? Bah! The only gold over there is the gold the London Company is wasting on the settlement!"

"At first," Newport said, "some of the London Company tried to hope the first assay was wrong. Perhaps the assayers were in the pay of Spain—denying we had found gold, until the Spaniards could send an armada to conquer Virginia. But we had another assay. The earth was worthless. The truth was a bitter dose. So far, the London Company had not made a penny of profit on the Virginia Colony. Instead, they would have to raise more money, and send out a supply. I tell you, I didn't enjoy facing them."

"But there will be profits!" Captain Martin insisted. "We will find gold! And we'll find the passage to the China Sea, too!"

"I know." Newport sighed. "I told them that. But we had a very stormy session. A third of the company were ready to wash their hands of the whole thing. They said that, hereafter, they would invest in the East India Company."

Ratcliffe's eyes blazed. "So they argued about their precious profits while we starved! Why didn't you tell them we were starving?"

"Tell them? I spent weeks telling them! Why do you think I'm two months overdue? 'Those men are starving!' I said. And do you know what the answer was? 'If we don't watch our investments, we'll be starving, too.' "

Ratcliffe spoke through clenched teeth. "About that time, I'd have run a man through! I'd have—"

"Would you?" Newport's voice was dry. "Or would you have held your temper, and kept on pleading, until you got supplies for Jamestown?"

Ratcliffe did not answer.

"Finally, I got two ships, and two hundred settlers. I have one hundred and thirty on the *Frances and John.* Captain Nelson has—had—seventy men on the *Phoenix* and . . . most of the supplies."

"Then the first thing," John Smith said, "is to begin trading for food."

"The first thing," Newport insisted, "is to build houses. I cannot return to England until these new settlers have shelter. When the building is under way, then we'll trade and—"

"The time to trade won't wait on anything!" John Smith insisted. "The Indians are not good managers. They admit it themselves. They feast and are fat after the harvest; they grow lean and despised when the food runs out. Those are their own words. I say—go north to Powhatan's village now."

"Where you were held captive?"

"I left him on good terms."

Archer's smile was lopsided. "Haven't you heard Captain Smith's latest tale? About being saved by one of Powhatan's daughters? And adopted into the tribe?"

Newport blinked.

"It's a custom." John Smith spoke abruptly. "If a child asks for the life of a condemned man, he may be spared. This child—Pocahontas—asked for my life. Powhatan indulged her whim. That was all."

Archer's eyes narrowed. "If I were you, Captain Newport, I would not risk going to Powhatan's village until I knew what sort of bargain John Smith made with the tribe!"

"I made no bargain!" John Smith roared. "If I had wanted to live at ease, I could have deserted Jamestown and stayed there! But if I had wanted to live at ease, I'd have stayed in England, and never have come to Virginia in the first place! I made no—"

A watchman yelled, "Indians!"

Guns ready, matches lighted, they covered the gate and opened it, staring into the forest.

Pocahontas stood there, slim, dark, poised like some woodland creature. Behind her, a dozen stalwart Indians carried baskets of corn. Another had a deer over his shoulders.

"I'll parley with them," Ratcliffe said. "Keep me covered with your guns." He advanced, and put his hand on his heart.

Pocahontas spoke slowly, in English. "Gifts for our brother. Where is our brother?"

John Smith cocked an eyebrow at Archer. "Now that you have seen her, do you believe her?" And he walked through the gate.

Pocahontas saw him, smiled, and came running. "Our brother! We bring gifts!"

"Your English is good! Fine!"

She smiled, and entered the fort hand in hand with John Smith. Ratcliffe shrugged and followed with the Indians carrying the gifts.

She looked up earnestly into Captain Smith's face, and talked softly in her own tongue.

"What is she saying?" Archer asked. "Tell her to talk English."

"She does not know much English."

"Then translate what she is saying! We'll have no plots hatched around here!"

"She says that she will call me *father* and I shall call her my *child*. And . . ." His eyes twinkled. "The rest of it is just a child's prattle."

"Translate!" Archer demanded.

"She said that my beard is beautiful."

Captain Newport laughed and came to bend over her hand.

"Yes," Captain Smith said slowly. "The great Father Newport. He came. As I said. See—the great ship!"

Pocahontas stared, big-eyed, toward the sails of the *Frances and John*. She lapsed into her own tongue again.

Captain Smith translated. "She says I spoke true words. I have Great Medicine. I said Father Newport would come. He did. When she goes back, she will tell the great Powhatan. Also"—he grinned at Newport—"your beard is beautiful, too."

For the first time since he had arrived, Newport looked

cheerful. "Captain Smith, you have made a valuable friendship. When the building gets under way, we shall visit Powhatan and improve those relations still further! But first—the building!"

The back-breaking toil of felling, stripping, and splitting trees began, as they slapped together more thatched shacks. Six new houses . . . then a dozen. . . . Most of the new men still lived in the cramped quarters on shipboard. The laborers grumbled; the gentlemen complained. Another half-dozen houses. . . .

From sunup to early winter twilight David swung an ax with the best of them, and grinned to himself when his hands did not blister. Not even some of the new laborers could work as long as he could!

Sometimes when he crawled into his bunk, he ached until he could not sleep. But after a few days the aching wore off. In a week he slept so heavily that someone had to shake him awake in the morning.

Twenty new houses . . . twenty-one. . . . After supper David stumbled toward his bunk, half asleep when he reached it. That night he dreamed he was back in Powhatan's village, in the smoky hut. One Indian was holding him, and another fanned smoke in his face.

He wakened, choking, and saw a red glare through the slits of his hut, and struggled against the grip of a hand on his wrist. But someone dragged him to the floor, out of the hut, and jerked him to his feet.

"David! Wake up!" John Smith shouted. "Run for the gate! Jamestown is burning!"

CHAPTER TWELVE

"*Let Us Trade as Kings!*"

"DO YOU hear, David?" John Smith shook him again. "Jamestown is burning! Run for the gate!"

David gasped, gulped fresh air, and ran past the crackling roar of thatched houses, to join the men outside the gate, shivering in the snow. Matthew Scrivener staggered out, carrying Master Hunt over his shoulders, and let him slide to the ground.

"My books!" the minister begged. "Please let me go back! My books!"

"Hold him!" Mr. Scrivener shouted. "There isn't a chance of saving them!" He plunged back into the burning town.

The wind rose, fanning the flames until they leaped the forty feet from the burning houses to the walls of the fort. Red tongues licked the logs of the palisade, smoldered, then flared. The fire roared and showers of sparks began to fly. The able-bodied moved the helpless ones back out of range.

Captain Newport came out, carrying an unconscious man. He laid him down, then looked back at the town. He gave a startled yell. "The ships! All hands on deck!" For sparks were flying now toward the inflammable rigging of the ships.

Working with frantic haste, the men weighed anchors, cast off mooring lines, carried small anchors out in boats, and kedged the ships to safety.

Dawn came. The shivering men stared at the smoldering ashes. Everything they had sweated and slaved to build was gone; their storehouse with its new supplies was gone. Some of them stood with tears crawling down their smoke-blackened faces.

One man looked toward the ships, and then ran a glance over the company. David could read his thoughts. He knew what he was going to say before he said it. "Captain Newport, can we . . . will the ships? . . ."

"We'll build again!" Newport said.

"First," John Smith insisted, "we trade for corn!"

The council talked it over; building could not wait on trading; trading could not wait on building. They put Mr. Scrivener in charge of rebuilding Jamestown. Captain Newport ordered the *Discovery* and the shallop manned for a trading expedition to Powhatan's village.

"We'll find it's further by water than it is by land, David," Captain Smith remarked.

David's heart jumped. "I'm going to get to go?"

"You're a man I can depend on."

With copper to buy three hundred bushels of corn, they set sail. Captain Newport addressed them from the quarter-deck. "One thing—there will be no private trading. We have been warned about that. We must keep our rate of exchange with the Indians."

"What about Captain Smith?" one of the gentlemen growled. "He's brought something for personal trading. A—"

"I know all about that!" Newport said. "A pound or so of blue beads. They are not for trading, but a gift for Pocahontas."

The gentleman sneered. "Two pounds of blue beads for saving his life? Is that what his life is worth?"

Newport's jaw tightened. "Weigh anchor. Topmen into the rigging!"

They started their roundabout journey, down the James, into the Chesapeake, north to the mouth of the Pamunkey, and up that river. Twelve miles overland . . . it was going to be a good hundred miles by water!

Long before they reached Powhatan's village Indians came in log canoes to meet them, circled the ships, and escorted them up the river. When they anchored and went ashore, Powhatan was ready for the meeting, seated on his high, bedlike throne, with his dozens of tall warriors behind him, his women and children at his feet.

Captain Newport stared. "Why—he—he's magnificent! Kingly as a lion."

"And wily as a fox," John Smith muttered. His glance

roved over the women and children. David had been looking, too. He didn't see Pocahontas, either.

Newport smiled at John Smith's words. "I don't think
we'll have to worry about the 'fox' in him. You can be our
translator, can't you?"

"Well," John Smith drawled, "I had time to pick up
quite a few Indian words while I was—a guest of Powhatan." As he talked with Powhatan, he translated what
he said, and Powhatan's answers.

The great Powhatan was in a jovial mood. "Our brother
promised a grindstone and two guns."

Captain Smith laid his hand on his heart. "Your brother
offered you the finest guns he had in the fort."

"And the heaviest?" Powhatan asked, and he laughed.

So Powhatan was not angry! David felt a moment's
relief; then a chill crept up his backbone. He rememberd
Powhatan the morning he sentenced John Smith to die—
terrible one minute—laughing the next; it might be the
other way around now—laughing one minute—terrible
the next.

Powhatan had many questions about the great ship that
Captain Newport had brought to James Island. Where
did they find a tree big enough to carve such a ship? Where
did they find animals big enough to furnish skins for their
sails?

"We make the ship of many logs," Newport said. "We
make sails of tiny threads. Some day we shall teach you the
secret."

Powhatan shook his head quickly. "No. That will never
be. You and your people will go away, across the great

salt water. I and my people will stay here, in our land. We shall not meet again."

Silence crawled through the party of white men. Captain Newport and John Smith exchanged a long look.

"Tell him this," Newport said. He spoke, and John Smith translated. "We have made new plans. I told our king in England about you. He wishes us to stay here, and to live with you as brothers."

When John Smith had finished translating, a guttural murmur ran through the warriors behind Powhatan. For a moment the chieftain's face was terrible, and his eyes burned. He leaned back to mutter something to the man at his shoulder. The mutter passed along the lines of warriors. Silence.

Suddenly Powhatan was pleasant again. "And you have come to trade with me?"

Newport released his breath in a gusty sigh of relief. "Yes, we have come to trade."

Powhatan made a sweeping gesture. "Then let us trade as kings—not as little men. Lay out what you have brought me, and I shall give you corn. Let us trade as kings—quickly. Then we shall feast!"

John Smith translated, and then muttered, "No!"

"But while he is in a good mood . . ."

"He is not! That 'good mood' is gone! Probably forever! This 'trading as kings' is a trick!"

But Newport gave orders, and his men placed the copper for three hundred bushels of corn before Powhatan.

Powhatan saluted him. "Truly, Father Newport is a king!" He swept his arm in a regal gesture. Some women hurried forward and set corn at Newport's feet—four bushels of corn. Powhatan's face was bland; only his eyes betrayed a glitter of amusement. Father Newport would understand, he said. Powhatan had very little corn, but he had given all he could spare.

Newport spoke through his teeth. "Why, that old . . . What are you going to say to him?"

John Smith gripped his arm warningly, smiled, and began to talk. They thanked Powhatan for his kingly gift. They sorrowed that he had so little corn. "I had hoped," he said, "that you would have enough corn to buy this greatest treasure that we have. It cannot be owned by every chief. Only the most kingly may own it."

Powhatan stiffened. "Who is more kingly than I? Ruler of thirty tribes? With two thousand warriors at my command?"

John Smith opened the pouch of blue beads, and lifted one bead in his fingers. "The mark of the kingliest of kings. Many kings have none. Even very great kings have only one."

Powhatan gave a guttural command. Two warriors brought a bushel of corn and set it at John Smith's feet.

The captain shook his head. The great Powhatan did not understand. The blue beads were very great treasures. When the Indians had brought five bushels of corn, he nodded.

"Because we are brothers, Powhatan, I shall let you have the blue bead for only five bushels of corn. In fact, because you are so poor, I shall let you have two blue beads. I am sorry my brother cannot buy enough beads to decorate all his family. Some other chief—not so kingly of course, but with more corn—will have blue beads to decorate all his brothers—all his women and children. But not the great Powhatan. I am sorry." He gave Powhatan the two beads and spoke to Newport. "Tell our men to load the corn . . . *and do it fast!*"

Newport hesitated. Only nine bushels? But he gave the order. They were halfway to the river when Powhatan's messenger came running.

"Our brothers will stay! We have found more corn!"

When the *Discovery* sailed, she rode low in the water.

Newport eyed John Smith. "And you called Powhatan 'wily as a fox.' What do you say of a man who trades two pounds of beads for two hundred bushels of corn?"

"Powhatan got value received; he has the copper, too, that you 'traded like a king.'"

Newport flushed and grinned ruefully.

Back at James Island, they found a new storehouse ready, but only three houses built. Two dozen men were sick of lung fever—pneumonia, Dr. Wotten called it—and five already dead.

"We must have houses to shelter our men!" the doctor said. "I've never faced such a winter!"

"And we must have a palisade." Captain Newport was grim. "Powhatan knows now that we intend to settle. The word will spread like fire. If the Indians attacked us now . . ."

"We must have food!" John Smith insisted. "We must trade now! The time is already late!"

"I think we should explore for gold," Captain Martin declared. "If we sent back gold to London—"

"No!" John Smith roared. "Not before the trading! Not before the building!"

Captain Newport shrugged. "Explore for gold if you want to—so long as you take only gentlemen with you. We need the workmen here on James Island."

Captain Martin and a few gentlemen departed. Captain Smith took another group in the shallop, to trade for corn. At Jamestown, the workmen slaved. Another month of brutal, back-breaking work, and they had rebuilt the palisade. But the men were still housed on the ships. Another two weeks and a few houses were slapped together. Not much protection against the cold, but better than tents. At this rate, though, it would take at least another month to have any sort of shelter for the whole company.

John Smith returned from his trading, took one look at the state of the building, and growled, "Let another man go for corn!" By the next day, men were seething under the lash of his tongue, but the building was getting on faster.

A shout hailed them from the mainland. Two of Captain Martin's party were waving and yelling. "Gold! We've found gold!"

The men felling trees dropped their axes; the men in the saw pits dropped their saws; the carpenters and joiners dropped their hammers and planes.

"Gold!" They swarmed out of the palisade.

"Stop!" John Smith roared.

A man shoved past him. "Didn't you hear? Gold! We've found gold!"

"Then we'll send a barrel to London," the captain yelled, "to be assayed. But we can't—"

A man laughed. "A barrel! We'll ballast the ship!"

"No! Stop! We must build houses! We must—"

But the cheering men did not stop. They grabbed picks and shovels and made for the mainland.

"Stop!" But John Smith was shouting at an empty fort and a handful of houses.

"Gold!" The cry echoed through the forest. "Gold!"

CHAPTER THIRTEEN

"Get the Grave Ready!"

APRIL—twelve weeks since Newport had arrived in Virginia. Still men filled sacks, casks, and barrels with the gold-showing dirt, and stowed them in the hold of the *Frances and John*. David was helping bend on new sails when Newport and John Smith came aboard.

Newport watched another barrel being lowered into the hold. "When I get back to London, ballasted with gold ore, our troubles will be over."

"If you get back with gilded dirt," John Smith growled, "our troubles have just begun. A barrel of ore would have been enough for an assay. We could have sent a cargo of cedar and clapboard."

Newport frowned. "The London Company did not think much of the 'taste of clapboard' we sent."

"They thought even less of the fool's gold, didn't they?"

Newport did not answer. "I'm taking Wingfield and Archer back with me. With them out of Jamestown, perhaps you'll have less quarreling."

"Perhaps. I can think of another one or two you could take with you."

"You might try getting along with them—not being quite so—so—"

"Well? Go on." Silence. John Smith grinned. "When Archer leaves, we'll need a recorder. How about David Warren?"

Newport's eyes widened. "That lad? Has Jamestown become 'a place for women and children'?"

John Smith laughed with him. "Childhood isn't a matter of years. David's handy with his pen, and a man I can depend on."

"Good!" Then Newport's smile disappeared. "We can do with a few dependable men—of any age."

The second week in April the *Frances and John* moved sluggishly downstream, heavy-laden with gold-showing dirt. Captain Martin gazed after her with shining eyes. Captain Smith cast one look after the ship, and turned back to the neglected work of Jamestown. The winter had taken a bitter toll; less than a hundred men had survived. There were still not enough houses to shelter them. But spring had come; fresh green clothed the bare trees; flowers carpeted the earth.

"Earth's only paradise," George Percy had called it, just a year ago. It looks that way again, David thought. If you can forget the summer's heat, and the swamp fever . . .

The men were cheerful. "We'll get on with the building now!" one promised. "Now that it isn't so cold!"

"You'd better," John Smith said, "before it's too hot."

All the laborers were hard at work, and the gentlemen were giving less advice than usual, when a watchman shouted, "Sail ho-o-o-o-o!"

The men swarmed to the gate. Had Captain Newport had trouble and returned? No, the watchman reported, it was not the *Frances and John*. It was a strange ship—but flying English colors.

"Man the guns!" John Smith bellowed.

When the ship drew nearer, the watchman challenged her.

A cheery voice answered, "The *Phoenix!* Captain Nelson commanding!" Men stared at each other.

The *Phoenix?* Caught in a storm months ago? It couldn't be! But it was. Captain Nelson brought his ship to anchor, and his men came ashore, laughing.

President Ratcliffe called the council—and David Warren, recorder—to hear Captain Nelson's report.

"The storm drove me clear back to the West Indies," he said. "But I didn't lose a man. And I didn't use the stores I was bringing to Jamestown. I traded with the natives there for food. I've brought seventy settlers. Can you house that many?"

"The building is a little behindhand," Ratcliffe admitted. "We found gold, and—"

"If it is gold," John Smith said.

"We can settle that question," Captain Nelson promised. "I've a gold refiner on board—Thomas Barren."

"A master," John Smith asked, "or just an apprentice?"

Captain Martin jumped to his feet. "He's a master! I've heard of Thomas Barren! Maybe his word will satisfy you!"

When Thomas Barren was ready with his report, the council met again. "I'm afraid I have bad news," he said. "It does not seem to be gold."

"What do you mean?" Martin asked. "Doesn't *seem* to be gold? It either *is* gold or is *not* gold."

"I mean, sir, it is not gold."

"You're sure?" Captain Martin strode toward him threateningly. "If the assayers in London say that it is gold, you know what will happen to you?"

Mr. Barren blinked. "Why should anything happen to me, sir? If I am wrong, it is just an honest mistake."

"Oh, no! If you've lied to us, it's not 'just an honest mistake.' You'd do that for one reason—because you're in the pay of the Spanish! Because they bribed you to lie about it! If the assayers in London say it is gold, you will be hanged for treason!"

John Smith cocked an eyebrow. "And if the assayers in London agree with him?"

Captain Martin spoke through his teeth. "I believe it is gold! And when the *Phoenix* sails, we'll ballast her with gold ore, too!"

"If we value our necks," John Smith said, "we'll load her with cedar. We have had the word of a gold refiner— a master, according to you—that it's fool's gold. If we—"

Captain Martin threw up his hands. "All right! We'll load cedar! But—if Barren is wrong—remember, John

Smith, that you were the man who insisted on loading cedar!" He stamped out of the meeting.

Mr. Scrivener looked after him, puzzled.

"He's a sick man," John Smith said. "Never has recovered from the swamp fever of last summer. The summer here—you can't believe what it's like until you have lived through it."

"Not worse than the winter!" Captain Wynne said. "We've lost a third of our men since January!"

"We lost two-thirds of our men last summer. Just thirty-eight survived."

Captain Wynne and Mr. Scrivener stared at each other.

Captain Smith stood. "Well, no use sitting around talking, is there? We've work to do!"

All through May David swung an ax, helping load the *Phoenix* with cedar. At night he worked with John Smith, making a copy of a long letter the captain was writing to a friend back in London.

"By the time Wingfield and Archer have told the story of Jamestown their way," the captain said, "I'd like to have one record of the truth of it in England. So that is what this letter is going to be—a true relation of our first year in Jamestown." Then he added dryly, "That is, as much of a true relation as we can tell—without saying anything to discourage other settlers from coming."

One year in Jamestown. . . . Time and again, as David sat copying the letter, he shook his head, unbelieving. How could all these things have happened in one year?

Once he stopped writing. "About our trip to the Ke-

coughtans, sir, for corn in November. Remember how
you captured their god, Okee, and stopped their attack?
That was a piece of the quickest thinking I ever saw.
You've forgotten to put it in."

"I did not forget."

"But—but—"

"Do you think that would encourage other settlers? To
know we had to trade for corn at the hazard of our lives?
Besides, when I did that I was disobeying orders; we are
'not to offend the natives.' "

"But we *had* to get corn! It was that or starve!"

"Yes . . . I did what I had to do—no more—no less.
But the fact remains that I was disobeying orders."

"But, sir—"

"Your job," the captain snapped, "is to make me a fair
copy of my letter! Get to work!"

"Yes, sir!" David clenched his teeth and started copying
again. I won't say another word, he told himself, no matter what he leaves out. Not another word!

He came to the part about Christmas at Powhatan's
village; no mention of the fact Powhatan ordered John
Smith put to death; no mention of Pocahontas.

"But, Captain Smith!"

"Well? What now?"

"Nothing, sir!"

"I thought not. Finish that page, and then to bed with
you. We've more cedar to load in the morning."

In June the *Phoenix* was ready to weigh anchor. Captain Martin was to return on her, leaving four men on
the council—President Ratcliffe, John Smith, and the two

newcomers—Mr. Scrivener and Captain Wynne. The night before the *Phoenix* sailed the council talked long and late. What word could they send to the London Company? If the ore that Newport carried was gold—well and good. But if it was another load of fool's gold—and a whole shipload at that—what then?

"I think we'd better tell them we are exploring for the route to the China Sea," President Ratcliffe said. "No more about gold until we have heard from that last assay."

The council agreed. They voted that John Smith should explore the Chesapeake Bay and the other great rivers to the north of them. Surely there they would find an easier passage to the China Sea than past the falls of the James River.

"And I'll chart the bay and the rivers," John Smith said. "We'll need a map of them." He looked at David. "I'll take our recorder with me. He's a fair hand at surveying."

"That so?" Ratcliffe looked surprised. "Odd thing for a boy to know. But take him along." He smiled. "We'll depend on you to choose your other men, too."

When word spread that Captain Smith was to explore the Chesapeake and the rivers north, men begged to go. Sailing up the Chesapeake would be far easier than working in Jamestown, felling trees and building houses! The captain could have had enough men to handle a vessel of a hundred tons. He chose twelve men and set sail.

James Gray, a dashing fellow who had come on the *Phoenix*, and two others of that group were among the dozen men who sailed in the shallop. Gray stretched, breathed deep, and smiled at David. "*This* is the expedition that will find the route to the China Sea! We're not turning back, as Newport did at the falls of the James! You know, you first settlers must have been a sorry lot. You have been in Jamestown more than a year, and what have you accomplished?"

For a long time David was silent, remembering. "We have survived—some of us. We have learned a few things not to do."

"Hah! Quite an accomplishment! Well, we on the *Phoenix* lived through the worst storm that ever swept the Atlantic! And we all survived! We're going to put some spirit in this colony! In this expedition, too. You know, there are three of us from the *Phoenix* in this boat. If your captain loses his nerve, and wants to give up, he'll have us to reckon with."

Into the Chesapeake they sailed, and crossed it to the eastern shore. Now a south wind was with them, speeding them north along the eastern shore of the bay. Bright sun on blue water, and a fair wind abaft the beam. James Gray smiled again. "This is the life for an Englishman!"

That afternoon clouds hid the sun, and the wind freshened, raising oceanlike waves in the gray waters of the bay. Then the rain came. For a week the twelve men lived in wet clothes, slept on the wet ground, and spent their days at the oars, fighting head winds. Time and again a wave washed over the shallop and set them bailing frantically.

James Gray shivered and scowled. "How much longer will this keep up?"

"Hard to tell," David said. "This is one of the things we survived our first summer. The storms."

Another week of storms, and James Gray was pleading with John Smith. "We can't go on in this weather!"

"Why not? There is nothing ahead of us that is any worse than what we have gone through."

"But how much longer . . ."

"Do we go on? Until we find a route to the China Sea!"

At last the rains ended. They crossed the northern end of the bay, to the western shore, where they had word of another great river, the Potomac. They reached the mouth of the Potomac and gaped in amazement. What a mighty river! Compared to it, even the Thames was a mere rivulet. At last they had found a river great enough to carry them to the divide and the passage to the China Sea!

Fifty miles—a hundred miles—on and on up the river they sailed. Then once more they heard the sound of a tremendous roar. Once more they found the river plunging over mighty cliffs that blocked their way.

"But—but—that's impossible!" James Gray said. "Only a madman would try a portage past those falls."

"Maybe that is what Captain Newport thought when he saw the falls of the James," David suggested.

For a long time they studied the mighty cliffs. Was there a divide just beyond these falls? And—five or six days' journey beyond—the China Sea? Perhaps . . . but perhaps they could find an easier passage to the westward-flowing river. So down the Potomac again, into the Chesapeake, and south to the next great river below—the Rappahannock. Would they find an easier passage there?

As they neared the mouth of the Rappahannock, the

shallop stopped with a suddenness that sent them sprawling. They had run aground.

David watched the motion of leaves floating in the water. An ebb tide. They would have to wait until the tide turned to float them off.

A confusion of shouts rose from the men: "Shove ahead—we'll get over the shoal! . . . No, push back, or we'll go deeper aground! . . . Get out! if we lighten the boat . . ."

The babble of voices stopped with a gasp, for John Smith had whipped out his sword. But the captain was paying no attention to the shouts. Leaning over the side of the boat, he stabbed down into the water.

"Got him!" He lifted his sword with a struggling fish skewered on it.

In a moment all the men had whipped out their swords, and were shouting and laughing as they stabbed fish, too. Some waded ashore to an island and started a fire to roast the fish.

"Make room for this one!" John Smith lifted his sword high with the biggest fish yet—an odd-shaped one, flat as a plate.

David saw the whiplike tail lash savagely. "Watch out!"

Too late. The tail lashed across the captain's wrist; he gasped as he dropped the fish on the pile of their catch.

Dr. Russell stopped fishing and sheathed his sword. "Captain! Are you hurt?"

John Smith winced as he rubbed his wrist. "It'll stop stinging in a minute."

"I've heard of a sting ray," Dr. Russell said. "If it's that,

the wound may be serious." He eyed the captain's hand. Soon it had swollen until his fingers were stiff. "Get that sleeve off while you can!" He helped the captain strip to the waist. The whole arm was swelling now. "I don't like the looks of that."

"I don't like the feel of it," John Smith muttered.

James Gray stared at the swelling arm. "Doctor, you've got to do something! How'd we ever get back to Jamestown if he—if the sting of the fish was—"

John Smith snorted. "Don't be a fool! It would take more than the sting of a fish tail to kill me!"

Two hours later the captain was not roaring; his arm had swollen to the size of a man's leg; his body was swelling, too. When he spoke, his words came slowly. "Is the tide going out?"

With a shiver David remembered the old superstition— that a man dies on the ebb tide. The others were remembering, too. He could see it in their eyes.

"It's turned!" one said quickly. "It's beginning to come in!"

John Smith spoke more slowly. "Then listen to me . . ."

Dr. Russell interrupted. "Captain, don't try to—"

"I'm giving the orders!" Even his whisper was a command. "David, you're a man I depend on. You will carry out my orders exactly. Do you hear?"

"Yes, sir."

"Two of you go now, over there beyond that tree. Dig a grave and have it ready."

"No, Captain! You—"

"Don't waste time! You must sail when the tide floats

us off. Get the grave ready. When I die, strip me and bury me quickly. Smooth the dirt well. Leave no mark of a grave. Go."

The men looked at each other. Dr. Russell shrugged hopelessly. Two men picked up shovels and walked away. The doctor muttered to himself, searched through his kit of medicines, and picked up a jar of salve. "I don't know if this could help."

The captain's eyes were dazed, but his lips twisted in a smile. "It can't hurt."

The doctor slashed open the place of the sting, and slathered salve on the wound. The captain lay quiet now, with closed eyes. Sweat drenched his hair and beard. The men who had dug the grave returned. Their eyes asked questions.

The doctor said, "No . . . not . . . yet. . . ."

CHAPTER FOURTEEN

Final Orders from London

JAMES GRAY shivered and spoke through chattering teeth. "He was harsh, but I'll say this for him! He was one of the bravest men I ever—"

"Don't say *was!*" David's voice shook. "He isn't dead!"

The hours passed; the incoming tide floated the shallop. They dragged it off the shoal, anchored it in deeper water, and returned to their watch.

At last a long-drawn sigh from the captain. Was it the end? Then he stirred, grimaced, licked his lips, and opened his eyes.

"Did you dig it?"

The men nodded.

"Too bad. We have enough necessary work. How's the fire? A good bed of coals?"

"Yes, Captain."

"Then roast that fish! I'm going to eat it!"

The cheers of the men sent birds screaming into the air.

The captain sat up, and shook his head groggily. "I certainly learned my lesson."

The doctor smiled. "About sword-fishing?"

"No. About keeping my charts up to date. If I had died, a lot of work would have gone for nothing. We need a map of this whole region, and of every river flowing into the bay."

By September, when they got back to Jamestown, twelve men in an open boat had traveled over three thousand miles; they had met many tribes of Indians—making friends here—barely escaping death there; John Smith had charted the Chesapeake and its great rivers, from Cape Charles on the south to the Susquehanna, far to the north. But they had not found gold; they had not found the route to the China Sea. Three months—half the time in sweltering heat or drenching rain—three months of facing the unknown day after day, never knowing if death waited in the next minute. Three months of danger and sweat. But they knew the London Company would not be pleased.

The London Company would not be pleased when they heard of the state in Jamestown, either; again the summer heat and the swamp fever had taken their toll. Once more disgruntled men had deposed their president. Ratcliffe, they said, had wasted their stores, and Ratcliffe had wasted their strength, building him a fine house in the woods. So—another president deposed; they had elected John Smith.

Ratcliffe shrugged and spread his hands. "I wish you joy!"

That evening, before a mass meeting, John Smith repeated the oath:

"I, John Smith, elected president for His Majesty's council for the first colony to Virginia . . ."

Listening, David swallowed hard, and blinked his eyes, even while he wanted to cheer. Less than two years ago, John Smith had arrived in Virginia in chains—a man disgraced. Now, he had been chosen for the highest office in the colony. *To overcome is to live.* The captain must be a happy man tonight!

But John Smith's eyes were stern, his voice was harsh, as he finished the oath:

". . . and generally in all things I shall do as a good and faithful servant and subject ought to do unto His Majesty, so help me God."

When he had taken the oath, he addressed the men of Jamestown. "I have been chosen to lead you in a hard fight—not only against savage tribes, but against the elements. Some of you have survived two summers here. You know what that can mean. Some of you have survived one winter here. You know what that can mean. But the summer is over, and the winter has not come. Now is our time to work with a will and build Jamestown! We do not know when Captain Newport will be back with a second supply. But when he comes, we must be ready for him and for new settlers. We must have houses built. And before we do that, we must enlarge the fort."

One of the gentlemen nodded. "An excellent idea! I've often said our quarters are very cramped. I can't see why in the first place you didn't build—"

"You'd like to help enlarge the fort?"

"Fine, President Smith! I'll take charge of the workmen and—"

"I mean," the new president said, "that you will take charge of an ax."

The gentleman smiled. "An ax? My dear man, I've never done manual labor in my life!"

"An ax," the president said, "to fell trees, or a pick and shovel to dig the ditch for the enlarged fort."

"But, my dear man—"

"We have work to do," the president said. "Forty workers cannot care for a hundred idlers. I'm asking the council to vote on this suggestion: Hereafter, every man shall work."

"Aye!" Mr. Scrivener and Captain Wynne spoke together.

Ratcliffe's face was blank with astonishment. At last he nodded. "Aye."

"It has been voted by the council," John Smith said. "Hereafter, he who does not work shall not eat."

The gentleman's amused smile was gone. "Please! Listen to me! I—" The rest of what he had to say was drowned in shouts of laughter from the workmen.

The captain's face relaxed. He even smiled at the gentleman who had "never done manual work."

"You'll get along all right, I'm sure. Of course, there are some tuffety-taffety gentlemen here who will find it hard to do a man's work. But if any gentleman feels he is not equal to a man's work, he may ask for another of his ilk to help him."

There was another roar of laughter from the laborers. When the meeting ended, the men of Jamestown did not separate into many little huddles, with six opinions being aired in as many groups. They broke into two factions— the laughing workmen and the fuming gentlemen.

The next morning when work began, the gentlemen were swinging axes with a savage concentration. Their president said nothing more. He was swinging an ax, too.

By mid-October, the change was unbelievable; a pentagon-shaped fort gave Jamestown twice as much room; inside were a dozen new houses. They had even dug a well to give them better water than the brackish, slimy water of the James.

Every Saturday afternoon all work stopped, and Captain Smith drilled his men. On the drill ground, the gentlemen had their chance to shine; they were excellent marksmen. After the first Saturday, Indians gathered to watch—a few, then more than a hundred.

John Smith smiled over that. "A little expert drilling in front of the Indians may save us many a fight. If we show them enough power, we'll not have to use it against them."

A new problem faced them in October; now was the

time to trade; yet building could not stop. They must divide their company for trading and building, and work harder than ever.

"Sail ho-o-o-o-o!" from a watchman warned them of a ship. Another shout gave them the good news. It was Captain Newport.

David helped man the boat that carried President Smith out to meet the ship; when they reached it, he climbed up the ladder behind the captain.

Newport wrung John Smith's hand, asked news of Jamestown, and introduced a new member for the council —Captain Waldo, a man as tall and brawny as David's father had been.

"We've brought some livestock this time," Newport said. "Sheep, goats, hogs, chickens, even horses."

John Smith wrinkled his nose, then grinned. "So I noticed." He studied the new settlers on the deck, and his grin faded.

"And I've brought a different sort this time," Newport said. "Not so many gentlemen."

"I see . . ." John Smith wheeled, leaped down to the main deck, and strode toward a roughly clad fellow. "Hold out your hands!"

The fellow smiled uncertainly, then thrust out his right hand. "I heard you need workmen, sir."

"Both hands!"

The fellow hesitated, and finally held out his left hand, too. John Smith looked, muttered, and turned to another man. Five times he challenged a man; five times the men held out only their right hands, until he roared, "Both hands!"

John Smith growled something under his breath, and turned to glare at Newport. Puzzled, David watched. What in the world was it all about?

They anchored the *Mary and Margaret*, and the newcomers swarmed ashore. The council came aboard to meet in Newport's cabin.

John Smith's first question was, "Where'd you pick up those settlers? From the jails?"

"What do you mean?"

"Didn't you look at their hands? How many of them are branded on their left thumbs? Thieves! Where'd you get them?"

"I don't have the choosing of the settlers! My job is to bring them over!"

"Who did choose them?" the president bellowed. "Who decided the scum of London could build a colony?"

"There aren't so many of them," Newport said.

"How many?"

"The way the London Company explained it to me," Newport said, "these men have made their mistakes—yes —but we're giving them a chance to made good. Get them away from their evil companions, away from the temptations of London, and—"

"Bah! If neither God nor shame could make them good in England, what will make them any better over here?" John Smith stood and glared down at Newport. "When the Spanish Armada threatened England, and we had to fight for our lives, did we empty the jails to man our ships?"

"Of course not! But—"

"Well, we're fighting a grimmer battle here than we've

ever fought before! And we can't win this fight with failures!"

Newport was on his feet, too. "So we need men who are successful. But tell me—why would a successful man come to Virginia? If a man has his house, his wife, his child at home—why would he leave them?"

John Smith blinked thoughtfully and sat down. "You know," he admitted, "I never thought of that." He sighed. "So we have to win this fight with failures." He looked up, pleading. "Confound it, Newport, you've been here! You know what we're up against! Can't you make the London Company see—"

Newport flared. "Perhaps you'd like to trade jobs with me? Maybe you'd like to face the London Company? Maybe you'd like to explain to them why we are asking them to spend money hand over fist with no return!"

"But," Ratcliffe said, "we loaded the *Frances and John* with—"

"Fool's gold!" Newport glared at John Smith. "Well, go on and say it."

"I'm sorry," John Smith said. "I know it hasn't been easy for you."

Newport snorted. "You may think you know." He looked around at the council. "Gentlemen, the London Company simply does not have money to squander with no return! They are teetering on the brink of ruin! This supply—and these settlers—may be the last help we'll get from England. Either we pull ourselves together, show them some real profit, or we're through."

Silence. The council stared down at the table.

Finally John Smith leaned back in his chair. "All right. That's what we face. Succeed now, or it's the end. How many of these—choice specimens of England manhood—did you bring?"

Newport's anger flared again. "I brought one hundred and thirty men! And they aren't all branded on the left thumb."

"I'm sorry." John Smith held out his hand to Newport. "I have no right to blame you. I'll keep my temper. Here's my hand on it." He smiled.

Newport shook his hand, but he had no answering smile.

"Now, about supplies," John Smith said. "The *Mary and Margaret* is a ship of goodly burden. We'll thank God —and the London Company—for that. We'll need thirty-odd tons of supplies to keep these new men until next harvest. And for the ones who are here—"

The new man, Captain Waldo, blinked. "*What!*"

"About six hundred bushels of meal, a hundred and forty bushels of peas, a hundred and forty bushels of oat-meal, seventy gallons of oil—"

"We haven't got it," Newport said flatly. "Not anything like it."

"You mean you—" John Smith started to roar, then checked himself. "You don't even have supplies for these new men?"

"No."

"Then what in the name of—" Again he checked himself. "What did the gentlemen of London do? Send the ship in ballast?"

"We have some livestock, as I told you."

"Good. It won't mean much now, but if we care for it, some day it will. But what else did you bring?"

"A great deal of the cargo space is given up to a boat. In five pieces, ready to be put together."

"We brought the shallop in the *Susan Constant* and still had room for supplies."

"This boat," Newport said, "is no shallop. It's *big*."

The president jumped to his feet again, and took a turn in the cabin. He stood gripping the back of his chair. "When we need something bigger than the shallop, we have the *Discovery*." His knuckles whitened, but he spoke with icy courtesy. "Did the gentlemen of London say what we are to do with this—this—leviathan of the seas—after we put it together?"

Newport was just as cool. "We are not to put the boat together here. We are to transport it beyond the falls, to the westward-flowing river. Then we are to put it together, and sail down the river to the China Sea."

"A boat bigger than the shallop?" John Smith asked. "In five sections? And we are to carry it overland, beyond the falls of these rivers?"

"The way they explained it to me," Newport said, "the boat is big enough to be seaworthy after we reach the China Sea. They are sure we can find a way to carry it past the falls to—"

"Oh, we can! There's no doubt about that!" The council looked up quickly. John Smith leaned over his chair and spoke through his teeth. "We can burn it, and carry the ashes in a sack!" With a mutter of disgust, he jerked out his chair and sat down again. "Tell us, did the gentlemen of London have any more brilliant inspirations?"

Newport flushed. "I told you I had my orders! My final orders! If I had not accepted them, I would not have got this supply!"

"What supply?" John Smith asked.

"I don't set the policy!" Newport roared. "I'm just the shuttlecock in this game!"

"I know . . . I know . . ." The president of Jamestown rubbed his hand over his forehead. "What's the rest of it?"

"I am not to leave Virginia until I have done one of three things: I must find gold, or the passage to the China Sea, or some trace of the lost colony of Roanoke."

"The lost colony of Roanoke?" John Smith evidently forgot he did not mean to roar. "Between 1591 and 1603, Raleigh sent five expeditions to hunt for them! *Five!* It's more than a quarter of a century since they disappeared! Why in the name of—"

"Those are my orders! Gold, the China Sea, or Roanoke! Stay in Virginia until I find one!"

"Hmmm . . . I hope you like Virginia." Then the president shrugged, as though casting off hopeless thoughts. "So that is what we face: more than a hundred new settlers, without supplies to keep them. Thank heaven this is the time for trading. If we can get in six or eight expeditions before—"

"There is one thing we must do before we start trading," Newport said.

The president's fist came down on the table. "We can't choose our time for trading! We must trade now."

Newport's fist came down, too. "Not until we have carried out this order! I have presents for Powhatan. We are to visit him in state, take him the presents, and crown him Powhatan I, Emperor of the Indians and loving subject to King James." He smiled wryly. "And you have my permission to roar again."

But for a long time the president was silent. At last he said, "Maybe if we go overland, we won't lose too much time."

"We can't carry these presents overland. We must go by water."

John Smith jumped to his feet again and started to roar. He stopped. At last he said, "I'll go overland with a few men, and invite Powhatan to Jamestown for the ceremony."

Newport frowned. "Have you been back since my visit? When we told him we are settling here?"

"No."

"You think you'll be safe with a handful of men?"

"I'll ask for volunteers." David looked up quickly. The captain nodded.

Newport said, "Do you think that's a trip for a boy?"

John Smith cocked an eyebrow. "David went to Powhatan's village once—by himself. When I was a prisoner there. Courage doesn't seem to be a matter of age. As I remember, most of the men of Jamestown were ready to desert the—"

"Take him, I say!" Ratcliffe spoke quickly. "And now, what about the livestock?"

John Smith bit back a smile. "That *is* a question, isn't it?"

They talked over the matter of livestock; they decided they would take the hogs to an island below Jamestown to fend for themselves, and build pens and shelters for the rest of it.

The meeting ended. Still muttering, John Smith called for volunteers for the overland trip to Powhatan's village. When the men reached the Pamunkey River, three of Powhatan's men were waiting to ferry them across.

"Handy, isn't it?" Amos Todkill remarked dryly. "And it shows that Powhatan has a friendly feeling for us. . . ."

When they reached the north bank, near the village, John Smith spoke to their guides. "Give Powhatan greetings from his brother. Tell him I have come with a message for him."

When the Indians had gone, the white men built a fire and made camp. Darkness fell; no answer from Powhatan.

"You'll take the first watch with Amos, David," the captain said.

Amos checked his gun, reached into the fire, and lighted his match, blowing on the rope until it glowed. David followed suit. When his match glowed, he turned away from the fire, closed his eyes to accustom them to darkness, then stared into the black night. He held his breath to listen for a whisper of sound—the crackle of a twig. But Indians, if they attacked, made no sound, did they? His heart thudded, his mouth was dry, and his hands were sweating.

A wailing scream rose to a shout. In a moment the camp was surrounded by shadowy figures.

CHAPTER FIFTEEN

Powhatan Makes an Offer

THE sleeping men scrambled to their feet and reached for their guns. The shrieks about them grew louder and the shadowy figures drew nearer the circle of light. Then John Smith began to laugh.

Pocahontas and two dozen Indian girls, painted, decked with feathers, wearing horns on their heads, were serenading them. When the dance ended, they brought food and spread a feast. Pocahontas, smiling, sat by the captain. Powhatan, she said, was in another village. They had sent for him. He would be back in the morning.

The next day Powhatan greeted them with a pleasant face. But when he heard their invitation, he scowled. "A present from your king? Then bring it to me! I, too, am a a king! I shall wait seven sleeps for your coming. Then, if you have not come, I shall go, and you may hunt for me!" He stood, made a haughty gesture to show that the interview was over, and stalked away.

John Smith flushed and clenched his teeth. It was easy enough to read his thoughts: things had come to a pretty pass when a savage gave orders and Englishmen must obey. But what else could they do? "To Jamestown!" the captain growled. "March!"

Back at the fort he called the council together and reported. "My advice," he said, "is to forget the coronation and trade for corn!"

"But the London Company—" Newport began.

"When you get back, you may lay the blame on me."

"There is enough blame laid on you now," Newport told him. "Here's a letter they sent you. I—in all the confusion, I forgot to—"

"Or decided it was better to save it for later?" John Smith opened the letter, started to read, then folded it abruptly and thrust it in his pocket. "I'll answer that in writing!" He shrugged and stood. "Load the pinnace with your presents. We'll visit him in state."

Newport smiled with relief. "That's better! After all, we do have our orders. Might as well do it and have done with it."

"We won't 'have done with it.' We'll pay for this foolishness and we'll keep paying!"

They loaded the *Discovery* and the shallop, and sailed down the James on the roundabout voyage by water. When they arrived, Powhatan waited in state, surrounded by his warriors and his women and children.

Newport said, "We'll depend on you to make him understand, Captain Smith."

"I'll translate," John Smith said, "but I don't promise to make him understand that he's 'Powhatan I, faithful subject to James of England'! Powhatan isn't going to be a 'faithful subject' to any man."

When Captain Newport held out the crown and asked that Powhatan kneel, the old warrior straightened to his full six-feet-plus and glared. Two of his wise men helped by pressing down on his shoulders, until he bent his knees and lowered his head an inch or two. Newport had to pretend that was sufficient "kneeling" for a faithful subject of His Majesty, King James. He put the crown on Powhatan's head. The chieftain still glared.

He smiled, though, when the men began to bring presents; a large golden bowl, a huge bedstead, with handsome coverings. He was willing for them to remove his moth-eaten raccoon cape and put a red velvet cape around his shoulders. The men came from the pinnace, bringing the last present in a heavy chest.

When they opened it, John Smith took one look into the chest and wheeled. "No! Not those!"

"Orders from London," Newport said. "Twenty swords."

"Never! I've risked my life to keep from trading weapons for food! We can't give him swords!"

"But this is not trading. These swords are a present."

"You think he'll know the difference? When we want to trade for corn?"

Newport shrugged. He had his orders. They presented

the twenty swords. Powhatan's eyes glowed. He made a long speech; he swept his hand in a majestic command. A warrior came with stately tread and presented a gift to Newport—from Powhatan I, Emperor of the Indians, to James I, King of England—the Indian's moth-eaten raccoon cape.

Newport flushed. "Tell that old—"

"We'll thank him," John Smith said. "And when you get back to London, tell the London Company what we got instead of the corn we need."

"We'll trade for corn now," Newport said.

But Powhatan shook his head. This was no day for trading. This was a day to feast and make merry. He ordered a feast spread, and songs and dancing. Before the feast ended, Powhatan had disappeared.

"No corn here," John Smith said. "We'll go on up the Pamunkey."

Newport insisted on returning to Jamestown. He had his orders. He must go up the James now, to take the boat past the falls and find the passage to the China Sea. As he returned from that expedition, he'd trade for corn.

When they returned to James Island, he loaded the *Mary and Margaret* with one hundred and twenty men, and sailed up the James. One hundred and twenty of the best men, of course. They would need strong men to succeed on that expedition!

John Smith looked at the men who were left, shrugged, and divided them into two groups—half to make clapboard to load the ship for its return to England, half to trade for corn.

Two weeks passed; Newport had not returned. Perhaps he had found a path beyond the falls. Another week; the men began to smile. No doubt about it! Newport had found the passage to the China Sea! Right now he was probably sailing down that westward-flowing river, toward all the riches of Cathay!

Four weeks . . . and the *Mary and Margaret* limped into port, with scarcely enough able-bodied men to work ship. Half the men had to be carried ashore. Ninety of the hundred and twenty were sick or injured.

No, Newport admitted, they had not found the passage to the China Sea; it was impossible to get through the rugged country beyond the falls. No, they had not found gold. No, they had not been able to trade for corn.

"The only thing now," he said, "is to search for some trace of the lost colony of Roanoke."

"The thing now," John Smith roared, "is to load your ship with clapboard and get back to England! And when you get there, face the London Company with a few simple truths! It's time they understood what we're up against in Virginia!"

"I've tried to tell them! If you think you can do better—"

"I'm writing a letter to them. An answer to their letter to me. It's going to tell them quite a few things!"

At night, when the day's work was done, David sat in John Smith's cabin, copying the letter he was sending to England. David never saw the letter from the London Company, but he could guess what it must have said, as he copied the captain's answer:

I received your letter wherein you write that our minds are so set upon faction and idle conceits, and that we feed you but with *if's* and *and's* and hopes and some few proofs; and that we must expressly follow the instructions sent by Captain Newport; that the charge of the voyage amounts to near two thousand pounds, which, if we cannot defray by the ship's return, we are like to remain as banished men. To those particulars I humbly entreat your pardons if I offend you with my rude answer.

As for factions, unless you would have me run away and leave it, they must be—else the men would fly the country.

For the charge of two thousand pounds, we have not received the value of one hundred pounds. As for the quarters boat to be borne by the soldiers over the falls, Newport had one hundred and twenty of the best men he could choose. If he had burned her to ashes, one might have carried her in a bag; but as she is five hundred cannot carry her to a navigable place above the falls. . . .

There was more; much more. John Smith did not hesitate to say what he thought of any of their orders from London. When David had made the copy, the captain gave his original letter to Newport.

"Here! This is my rude answer to the London Company. Read it! You have a right to know what word you carry back to them."

Newport began to read and looked up quickly. "But you can't talk this way to the—"

"Have I said anything that is not true?"

"No . . . but . . ."

"Isn't it time they know the truth?"

Newport tried to reason. "Look! Wingfield and Archer are in London now, talking against you. And Captain Martin—after the dispute you had with him over the gold-showing earth—he's not saying good of you. The London Company is already irked with you. If you send them a letter like this—"

"That's my answer!"

"I know the mood of those men. I advise you—I beg you—don't send that letter."

"You have advised; I have heard; the letter goes."

Newport tried once more. "Did you know that Captain Ratcliffe wishes to return with me?"

"Take him."

"One more tongue to wag against you in London."

"Let it wag!"

Newport sailed; with him—Ratcliffe, and John Smith's "rude answer." In Jamestown, less than two hundred men, and half of those still recovering from the ill-fated expedition up the James. In Jamestown, a storehouse so ill-supplied that once more starvation threatened. In Jamestown, one survivor of the original council—John Smith; three other men on the council: Scrivener, Waldo, and Wynne. Four men and five votes. Soon the council was down to three men and four votes, for Captain Waldo, great, brawny man that he was, sickened and died as suddenly as Gosnold had died the first summer.

Again John Smith laid down the law, and the council stood back of him; those who did not work would not eat. Every man who could stand on his feet worked—some at building, some at trading for corn. But—trade as they did—supplies were still short. The priceless time for trading had been wasted on crowning Powhatan and hunting for the route to the China Sea.

In mid-December two Indians came with a message. Powhatan sent greetings to his white brother, Captain Smith. Powhatan wanted workmen to build him a fine house; if his brother would send workmen, Powhatan would load their boats with corn.

David had not realized how worried John Smith was until he saw the relief on his face.

The captain smiled when he sent fourteen men overland to start the house; he smiled when he ordered the pinnace and the shallop readied for the journey. He grinned at David. "Looks as though you might spend another Christmas with Powhatan."

Christmas. . . . The word brought David up short. Was it only two years ago he had floundered through the snow, trying to keep up with Jem? Was it only one year ago he had been in Powhatan's village, sitting in a smoky hut, beating out songs on a drum? Only last year that he had "overcome childhood"? He shot a glance toward the captain, to see if he was remembering, too.

But John Smith was thinking of something else. He pulled a string of beads from his pocket and watched them glitter in the sun. "A present for Pocahontas," he said. "The child never got her blue beads." Then he straightened and spoke crisply. "Check the pinnace, David. You'll be my first mate."

The next morning fifty men boarded the pinnace and the shallop. From the palisade, Captain Wynne and Mr. Scrivener waved good-by.

"Men to depend on in Jamestown," the captain said. He smiled at David. "A man to depend on with me."

On board, the men sang as they weighed anchor. Even when the breeze died and they had to break out their oars, they sang. On the shallop, George Percy's men started "Deck the Hall." The men on the pinnace picked it up, and rowed in time to their singing.

By afternoon, a numbing cold gripped them.

"Keep a sharp lookout for smoke," John Smith said. "We'll spend the night in the first village we see."

The quick winter dusk began to blot out the world, and there was no sign of a village. The men of the shallop began to worry. They could not spend the night without shelter. They'd freeze to death before morning.

George Percy hailed the pinnace. Should they turn back?

"Turn back?" John Smith called. "Because of the

weather? Don't worry! I've spent the night in the open when it was colder than this!"

"To hear him tell it," one man muttered, "he's done everything!" Still grumbling, he followed orders, as they anchored their vessels and went ashore. They gathered wood for three huge fires. When they had been roaring for an hour, the men scraped the fires to one side, and spread their mats and blankets on the ground where the fires had been. "Why . . . it's warm!" the grumbler said.

David grinned. "Of course. The captain must have done this before."

The next morning they battled head winds, then sleet that changed to snow. Soon they moved blindly in a world of whirling white. With lead line and pole they felt their way to anchorage and went ashore. They stumbled about, groping for each other.

John Smith shielded his compass from the snow and studied it. "This way," he said, "to the village of the Warraskoracks."

"You're sure?"

John Smith did not even bother to answer. He started off through the blinding snow. Half an hour later, the king of the Warraskoracks welcomed them to his village. The expedition sighed with relief, then gasped at his first question.

"You go to trade with Powhatan? Because he promised to load your boats with corn?" The white men exchanged quick glances. How had the chieftain known?

John Smith nodded. "We go to trade for corn."

"It is a trick," the Indian declared. "Powhatan will

speak fair words, but he intends to cut your throats. Do not go."

David studied the Indian's face, trying to read what was back of his eyes. Did he speak the truth? Was he their friend? Or was he their enemy, trying to make trouble between them and Powhatan?

"Do not go," the Indian said again. "He will put you to death."

"I have sent my men to build his house. I have given my word to them that I will come. If I do not come, those men will die."

"Then let a few men die! If you go, you and all these men with you will die." The white men stirred uneasily and looked at their captain.

He said again, "I have sent my men. I have given my word. I go."

The Indian smiled. "Before the storm ends, you will have time to think; you will have time to grow wise."

John Smith did not answer. He bargained with copper for shelter and food for his men. The Indians housed them in a huge, tunnel-like hut, with a fire burning in the middle of the floor. Smoke rose toward a hole in the roof, then, buffeted by the wind, swirled through the hut.

George Percy choked. "How long will this keep up?"

"You'll get used to it," John Smith said. "It helps if you lie down."

That night, in the hut, the silence grew heavy.

"I wonder . . ." George Percy said. "Which one do you believe? The Powhatan, or this chieftain?"

"I believe in myself! I'm going for corn, and I'll come

back with corn!" He set the watches, stretched out, and slept.

Christmas Eve came; the storm still held them prisoners. They ate a supper of smoked fish and venison. They sat and looked at each other.

"Two years ago," one said, "we were in the Thames. I remember—we expected to be in Virginia in six weeks. But it was—"

"And one year ago," John Smith said, "I was in Powhatan's village, expecting to die. And you had given up hope of Newport's return. That was our dark hour."

"But . . ."

"Let's sing!" John Smith shouted. " 'Wassail'!" They sang; the song ended; silence crept over them again.

If I were home, David thought, there would be a yule log and a boar's head, and . . .

"Let's sing!" John Smith ordered. " 'Deck the Hall'!" The song began haltingly, but soon they all were shouting. They sang it through twice. Once more silence.

"If I were home . . ." one said.

" 'Wassail'!" the captain shouted. "This time, let's make it ring!" They sang. Outside, the storm howled.

"Before the storm ends," the Indian had said, "you will have time to grow wise." Did he speak true words? What waited for them in Powhatan's village? Friendship? Or death?

CHAPTER SIXTEEN

Pocahontas Brings a Warning

NEW YEAR'S DAY came and passed before the storm ended and they said good-by to the king of the Warraskoracks.

"You go to the village of Powhatan?" he asked.

John Smith nodded. "We go."

"You will not live to come back."

"We go for corn, and we'll come back with corn." The captain gave his order. "To the river! March!"

Behind them, the Indians began a mournful dirge; the wail followed them through the forest.

One man shivered. "Listen to that! I wonder what they are saying?"

David had no trouble understanding; he had picked up

quite a few Indian words. But he did not offer to translate. "Probably just wishing us fair winds and good sailing," he said. "All their songs sound terrible. Remember, Captain Smith, when they serenaded us?"

The captain smiled. "I've an idea Pocahontas will serenade us again."

When they reached Powhatan's village, there was no sign of Pocahontas. Powhatan greeted them coldly.

"Why have you come with guns in your hands? Why do you not come as friends?"

"We have come as friends," John Smith said. "You promised corn; we have come to get it."

"I have no corn for men with guns in their hands. Come in peace, and I shall give you corn." His voice grew harsh. "You must lay down your guns!"

David felt a chill run up his spine. Powhatan, with sixty warriors behind him—and no one knew how many more lurking in the forest—Powhatan had delivered his ultimatum. What now? The men stirred uneasily and cast wary looks about them.

Only their captain seemed untroubled. "Powhatan, I have vowed my love for you. You have vowed your love for me. You asked me to build you a house. I have sent men to build it, even while my work must wait. Where is the corn you promised?"

"I have no corn!"

"Does my brother speak with a split tongue?"

Powhatan's eyes blazed at that. Then he controlled himself and spoke quietly. "Perhaps," he said, "a little corn. For thirty swords, I can give you thirty bushels of corn."

"We have no swords to trade."

"Father Newport brought me swords!"

David saw the captain's face harden; he remembered the warning; the present of swords would make trouble.

But when the captain spoke, his voice was quietly matter-of-fact. "I have no swords to trade. You asked for men to build a house. I have kept my part of the bargain. Where is the corn?"

Powhatan's sternness melted. He began to plead. "You shall have corn. But my people are afraid of your guns. When you lay down your guns—"

"Your people have no reason to be afraid of our guns. You have seen their power. You should know that if we meant to hurt you, we could have done it. I have given my promise to live at peace with you. I have done it. Where is the corn?"

Over and over and over again: *Where is the corn?* Would the captain's patience never end?

Powhatan grew stern again. "There is no corn for men who come with guns. *If you want food you will have to lay down your guns!*"

David's breath escaped in a shuddering sigh; his chest ached from holding it so long.

The captain shrugged. "We have kept our word; if we cannot depend on the word of Powhatan, we shall go."

Powhatan glared. "And you will starve!"

John Smith hooked his thumbs in his belt. "Oh, no! We won't starve! We have ways of getting corn that you know nothing about! We do not have to trade with a man who speaks with a split tongue!"

For a time Powhatan was silent; at last he spoke sadly. "I cannot understand you; I have called you *brother*. I have used you more kindly than any other. But all others are kinder to me than you are. Father Newport gave me presents. When Father Newport traded with me, he took what I gave and was glad." He held out his hands. "Let my brother believe! Let us live as friends. Send away your guns, and I shall load the boats of my brother."

"Maybe he really means it," George Percy whispered.

John Smith only said, "We never lay down our guns. We have kept our promise. Does Powhatan keep his promise? Or does he speak with a split tongue?"

The silence stretched. At last Powhatan gave commands. Indians began to load the boats with corn. The white men, still with their guns ready, watched. The brief winter day began to darken.

One of the new men nudged David. "Warren!" he whispered. "Something's up! Powhatan's disappeared!"

David tried to sound as unconcerned as John Smith would have sounded. "We're almost loaded. We'll be out of here before anything can happen."

A panting man came running from the riverbank. "Captain! The *Discovery* is aground! Not a chance to move until the tide floats us off!"

The man by David nudged him. "Hear that? Now what will we do?" David did not answer. He didn't know what to say.

John Smith spoke to an Indian. "Tell Powhatan his brother needs food and shelter for the night."

Once more they sat in a huge, smoky hut, coughed,

and wiped their eyes. Indians came with a message from Powhatan. He was sending a feast to his brothers. But would his brothers please put out their matches? The smoke made his Indians sick.

The captain glanced at the bit of slow-burning rope smoldering in his hand, and then at the smoke spiraling up from the fire. He was sorry, he said, but they never put out their matches. The Indians departed. Darkness was complete. No one brought food.

A man stirred impatiently. "Is he just going to let us go hungry?"

John Smith cocked an eyebrow. "I can think of worse fates. Can't you?"

Outside, the guard challenged someone. The curtain moved. A frightened Indian girl, with wide eyes and a pinched face, slid quickly inside. David gasped when he recognized her. Pocahontas! What could have changed her from the happy child who had visited them in Jamestown—who had serenaded them with her maidens?

Her frightened eyes searched the hut, and found John Smith. She hurried to him, knelt, and laid her forehead against his hand.

"Yes, Pocahontas? What is it?"

For a long moment she did not speak. At last she looked up. "This thing I do . . ." Her lips trembled. "This thing I do—it is against my people." Tears filled her eyes and she bowed her head quickly to hide them. "A great feast comes. They will call you *brother*. But while you are eating, they will kill you."

"Thank you, my child. And do not cry. They will not

kill us, because we will not lay down our guns. Do not be afraid." He brought the string of beads from his pocket and let them touch her arm. "Here, Pocahontas. A gift for you."

She shook her bowed head. "I cannot take them."

"Why not? You call me *father* and I call you my *child*. I bring a gift to my child."

"I cannot!" She was sobbing now. "My people would see. They would know I had warned you. They would kill me." She sprang to her feet, and ran to the doorway. For a moment she stood poised, listening. Then she was gone.

Presently ten strapping Indians came with food. They paused at the doorway. Would their brothers please put out their matches? The smoke made them sick.

John Smith stood. "Your brother is sorry. We never put out our matches. Thank Powhatan for this food. And give him a message for me. If he would visit me tonight, tell him to make haste. I am ready to receive him!"

The Indians looked at the guns and the slow-burning matches. Sullenly they set down the food and left the hut.

When the men had eaten, the captain posted guards. Though David was not of the first watch, he might as well have been, for all the sleep he got. None of the men were sleeping much, he decided. A crackling twig brought him to his feet. One of the guards from the *Discovery* slid into the hut. The pinnace was almost afloat. Silently they wakened the sleepers. Making no sound, they crawled from the hut on their bellies, and wormed their way toward the river. The moon was good to them; it did not come out of hiding until they were all aboard.

They weighed anchor. "Back to Jamestown?" one asked.

John Smith started, as though his thoughts had been far away. "No. On up the Pamunkey. To the village of Opekankanough. We must have more corn."

"But—" David said, then stopped. Opekankanough was the chieftain who had captured John Smith a year ago, and had taken him to Powhatan to be put to death.

The captain did not seem to notice that David had started to speak. He stood with bowed head. Presently he stretched his hand out over the water. The beads for Pocahontas glittered a moment, then fell. He straightened and spoke briskly. "Yes, we'll get corn there."

Opekankanough . . . David felt a knot twist in his stomach. Was John Smith ever afraid?

Opekankanough greeted them with fair words. He would gladly trade, he said. Much corn—for guns. Again the long parleying began. How many times, David wondered, had John Smith said "we have no guns to trade"? Over and over, always in that same tone. Didn't he get tired sometimes, and want to shout it? Restlessly David shifted his feet, let his glance rove, then smothered a gasp. Painted warriors, with drawn bows, stood behind every tree, surrounding them with a ring of death. John Smith must be warned! He had not seen the warriors! His eyes were on Opekankanough.

Erect but relaxed, the captain shook his head, saying one more time, "We have no guns—" Suddenly his hand shot out in a motion so fast it blurred, and he seized Opekankanough by his forelock, and held a pistol at his chest. His tone did not change. "Tell your men," he suggested, "that we have come to trade, not to fight."

At last Opekankanough smiled and spoke fair words again. It was a mistake, he said. His men did not understand. But they were friends.

John Smith smiled, too. He was glad they were friends. Did his friend have corn to trade? For copper?

Opekankanough shouted an order. The warriors disappeared. Other Indians began to carry corn to load the boats. When the shallop was almost full, David felt eyes boring into his back. Taking his time about it, he turned, and saw a shadow of movement as a head ducked behind a tree. A hand reached out to beckon—a white man's hand. What in the world? He meandered toward the tree and walked past it. Out of the tail of his eye he saw Tom Whiffen, one of the men they had left at Jamestown.

"Thank God I found you!" Tom said. "Tell the captain to get back to the fort as fast as he can! Everything's a hotch-potch!"

"Can't Mr. Scrivener and Captain Wynne—"

"They're dead. Both of them, and ten others. Ten of the best. Their boat was caught in a storm. Until the captain gets back, there is no one in charge at Jamestown! *No one!* He's the last of the council!"

David stared at him aghast. Heartsick, he returned to the riverbank. The Indians were loading the last of the corn into the shallop. Something in David's face must have warned John Smith. He ambled over and took David aside.

"If it's trouble, we can't show it. What's wrong?"

"Tom Whiffen came. Mr. Scrivener and . . ." His teeth began to chatter. He bit down hard for a moment and then went on. When David had finished, John Smith's head was bowed.

The captain straightened, slapped David on the shoulder, and called in a hearty voice, "Is the shallop loaded, Master Percy? I'll take it back to Jamestown, and let you trade for more corn to fill the pinnace." He stood on the riverbank, watching the pinnace get under way and move upstream. He waved a cheery salute. He turned, and the brisk cheeriness was gone. "Scrivener . . ." he whispered. "Matthew . . ."

On board the shallop, though, he said nothing of the loss. He seized an oar and forced the men to the pace he set. When they got back to Jamestown they found things, as Tom Whiffen had said, a hotch-potch. It was February now—six weeks since they had sailed down the James— three weeks since the boatload of men had died. All building had stopped. Men had even torn down some of the houses and used them for firewood.

"We heard you were dead," they explained, "and when the others were lost, and there was no council—"

David saw the truth of it hit the captain. Until Newport came again—if the London Company ever sent him again —the fate of Jamestown depended on one man.

"You have a council now," John Smith said. "A council of one man. The responsibility is mine, and the power is mine, to see that Jamestown survives. And it's going to survive! Make no mistake about that!"

"But we can't stay here and starve! While there's food enough we ought to go to the West Indies and—"

"Never! We're going to stay here, and we're not going to starve! I traded for corn with Powhatan. I—"

"But this time," one said, "you had to trade guns for corn."

"I did not trade guns!" he roared. "I'll never trade guns!"

The men stared, bewildered, and then looked uncertainly at each other. "But—but—you sent for guns! The Germans who are building Powhatan's house. They came. They said you had sent them for guns."

For a moment the captain was white with fury. Then he spoke slowly, quietly. "How many guns did you give them?"

Shamefaced, the men admitted they had given three hundred guns, swords, and hatchets to the Germans to take back to Powhatan. David watched the captain's eyes and waited for the roar.

But after a long silence the captain spoke quietly again. "So we have lost some weapons to Powhatan. And some traitors. But we have not traded guns. Powhatan knows that. He knows the only way to get guns is from traitors. And when the ammunition runs out," he finished grimly, "I should not want to be those men. But"—he straightened —"no other Indians have gotten weapons from us!"

Again the men exchanged sidelong glances. They weren't sure, they said, but they suspected the Chickahominies of a little—er—stealing. "They've been coming to see us," one explained, "very friendly-like. But every time, after they have gone, we miss something—a hammer, a pistol—an ax—"

"We'll put a stop to that!"

"But we've got to get along with the Indians, haven't we? We're not to offend the natives."

"There is a difference between getting along with them and showing them you are too spineless to stand up for your rights! We'll take care of that when the time comes! Now—back to work!"

Toward the end of February, George Percy returned with a good supply of corn, but a crew of silent, preoccupied men. "We've been wondering," Master Percy said. "I mean—well—we didn't leave Powhatan in a very good humor, did we?"

The captain snorted. "We got out alive; we traded for corn, without killing a single Indian or losing a single man!"

"I know . . ." George Percy was troubled. "But we've been wondering. Perhaps Powhatan really meant it when he said if we laid down our guns . . ."

"Hah! You saw Pocahontas when she came to us that night. Did you think she was lying?"

"But perhaps we had angered him with our guns. We've been wondering what would have happened if we had laid down our guns."

"So long as I'm in command, you'll keep on wondering. We will never—"

He stopped. Three Chickahominy Indians had entered the fort with small presents of smoked fish. Now there was confusion. One of the Indians had fled. Amos Todkill and a fellow soldier were grappling with the other two.

"I can't tell what he's saying," Amos panted.

Captain Smith strolled over to listen. "It seems their wicked, wicked companion took a pistol and fled. These two are brothers. And of course they had nothing to do with the stealing. Creatures with white hearts, both of them. If I will release them, they will run on wings of the wind to their village, and they will run on wings of the wind back again. They will not stop until they have returned the pistol."

"That sounds reasonable," Master Percy said. "And the Chickahominies have been friendly."

John Smith harangued the Indians long and sternly. "Hold your captive, Amos, and let the other go." The Indians pleaded wildly. At last the one fled. "I told him," the captain said, "to 'go and come on wings of the wind' alone. I also told him that if he is not back by tomorrow, his brother will die."

Master Percy gasped. "But we can't kill them! It's absolutely against the rules to—"

"Why should I kill him? One man carried the pistol away; one man can bring it back." He nodded toward a hut. "Lock him in there, Amos. Build a charcoal fire to keep him warm. See that he's fed."

George Percy shook his head. "I'm afraid we're piling up trouble for ourselves."

The men began muttering; it was plain that they agreed with Master Percy. They'd made enemies of their best friends! All over one miserable pistol!

All afternoon the mutterings grew louder—until the brother returned, and ran to kneel before John Smith with the pistol—two pistols, in fact—and a hatchet.

"He of the white heart," John Smith said, "is admitting that he was the thief of these other things." He swept an amused glance over the muttering men. "Amos, bring out the prisoner."

"Yes, Captain!" Amos saluted smartly, marched to the hut, flung the door open, and called. He waited. No answer. He called again. Silence. He looked inside. Then, with a sharp exclamation, he dived into the hut.

A moment later he backed out, dragging the limp body of the Indian. The brother, who had been kneeling before John Smith, leaped to his feet. He beat his chest and shook his fists at the sky, calling down vengeance.

Amos stared, white-lipped, at the body. "Dead, sir. From the fumes of charcoal. He had gone to sleep with his head practically in the fire."

CHAPTER SEVENTEEN

Captain's Orders!

THE brother's anger turned to grief. He lifted a keening wail that curdled the blood. John Smith knelt by the limp body.

Master Percy's face was grave. "I'm afraid he's done it now."

A flood of accusations began: "Killed an Indian over a pistol.". . ."Now we'll have trouble with the Chickahominies!". . . "The best friends we've had among the Indians!". . ."Why didn't he send both brothers after the pistol!". . ."Right! Why didn't he show a little faith in them?"

The captain looked up and talked to the brother. The

wild mourning stopped. The brother listened; he laid his hand on his heart with wild protestations. What in the world?

"There is still a faint pulse," the captain said. "Help me rub him. Bring me brandy." Four men knelt to help. The brother was still making vows, his hand on his heart.

"What is he saying?" George Percy asked.

"I asked him what he would do if I brought his brother back to life. He is promising he will steal no more. He is also confessing how many more things he has stolen— he of the white heart."

At last the "dead" man stirred, groaned, and opened his eyes. With a wild shout the brother knelt before Captain Smith, beating his chest, making more vows. When the man had recovered, the captain gave them presents and sent them on their way.

He cocked an eyebrow at Master Percy. "Well?"

Master Percy's smile was troubled. "I'm afraid we haven't heard the last of that."

"I hope not!"

George Percy stared, bewildered. "You—you—expect repercussions?"

"I do!"

Three days later half a tribe of Chickahominy Indians appeared, carrying guns, swords, hoes, hammers, and hatchets. One after another they advanced, knelt, and laid their burden at the captain's feet. When the last gun was on the pile, John Smith delivered a rousing speech. The Indians laid their hands on their hearts, bowed, and departed.

The captain touched the pile of weapons and tools with his toe. "Our dearest friends, the Chickahominies." He bit out the words. "Did you know how much they had stolen?" No one answered.

"What did you say when you sent them away?" Master Percy asked.

The captain grinned. "I said: You have seen how great is my power! Remember it!"

Some of the men laughed; others muttered. "Just luck." . . ."What if he hadn't managed to save the fellow?" . . ."If the man had died, we *would* have had trouble!"

If John Smith heard, he gave no sign. "Now," he said, "let's begin working!"

"But we have been working! As hard as—"

"You haven't even started working. From here on, you'll really work! You'll work, or you'll starve! Every last man of you!"

He organized them into working groups and trading expeditions. The face of Jamestown took on a magic change; sturdier houses now; two storehouses, bulging with corn; a new blockhouse on the neck of the land leading toward the shore; trained guards posted night and day.

By spring they had cleared and planted forty acres. There would be food this fall! And the second storehouse had not yet been opened; it held the corn that would feed them until they could harvest their first real crop.

At last even the men who had rebelled against John Smith's harsh rule began to cheer. They had done it! They had founded a colony in America and kept it going! Times had been hard—but they were over the worst part now! They had won!

When their captain proposed they build a second fort, on a higher point of land, he did not have to order men; they volunteered. The frown lines began to fade from between the captain's eyes. More and more often he smiled.

"You've done it, sir!" David said. "You've made a success of Jamestown!"

"Fate did it," John Smith told him, "by removing the council and giving one man the power—and the responsibility. In an emergency, a leader must make decisions. England has learned that that must be true on the high seas; on a ship, every man is under the absolute rule of the captain. We'll learn that about colonizing, too. By trial and error, perhaps." He smiled and gripped David's shoulder. "But we'll learn it!"

It was a morning in April when they cleared out the last of their first supply of corn, and the captain sent men to open the second storehouse. They unlocked the door, swung it wide . . . and a moment later the commotion brought half the men of Jamestown to see what was wrong. The men at the storehouse were shouting and laying about them with their swords.

Rats! Brought to Jamestown in the holds of the ships. They had battened on the corn in the second storehouse. Now, when the door was opened, they swarmed out by dozens—hundreds. Even before the men examined the casks of corn, they knew what they would find—utter destruction.

They stared at each other, appalled. In one moment

the picture had changed; instead of a comfortable plenty, they faced starvation. Wild-eyed, they began to babble suggestions: "Kill the livestock" . . . "Trade with the Indians . . . They surely have corn hidden away! If we offer guns . . ."

"Silence!" John Smith bellowed. "And listen to me! We cannot touch the livestock. Try to live off it now, and it would not last three weeks! And don't hope for any help from Powhatan! If you weaken, if you trade the first weapon for food, that is the end!"

"But how will we live?"

"We'll live off the land!" the captain declared.

He divided the men into groups, sending part downriver to live off the oyster beds, part to Point Comfort to fish, and part upriver to live off roots and berries.

A few of the sturdiest workmen he kept at Jamestown. "We have more to do than just to survive," he told them. "We must get on with the building."

"But how will we live?"

"The sturgeon are running now. We'll live off fish."

"We'd work better on meat," one suggested. "If we ran down to Hog Island and—"

"We'll not touch the livestock!"

"But we—"

"You'll obey orders!"

They glowered, but they obeyed. The building at Jamestown went on.

In July the watchman's shout sent them scrambling to the gate. A ship flying English colors anchored at Jamestown. Captain Samuel Argall came ashore and reported to President Smith. He had come on a double mission, he said—first to check the shorter route due west from the Azores, and second to fish.

He brought news of the London Company. Time and again, as Argall talked, David wanted to stand up and cheer. Evidently John Smith's "rude answer" had jolted the London Company into new action.

"A new day has dawned for Jamestown," Argall said. "Everyone is investing in the London Company. There will be plenty of money now. And we won't be sending settlers by the hundreds—but by the thousands! And no more business of a council sitting over here and bickering! They've appointed one man governor for life!"

"About time," John Smith said.

"Who?" David asked.

"Lord Delaware. He'll sail in August, with about a thousand settlers. Meantime, Sir Thomas Gates will come to act as deputy governor. Gates is probably on his way now, with nine ships, five hundred men, and a hundred women, children, and servants."

"And supplies?" John Smith asked.

"Don't worry about supplies! The penny-pinching days are over! They are going to make a permanent settlement here. They will have everything they need! Everything!"

"Everything but houses to shelter them," John Smith added. "We'll have to build faster."

Before Argall sailed, John Smith bought all he could of Argall's supply of beef and ship's biscuit. He called his men back from downriver and upriver.

With food on hand, and news of nine ships coming, the men were ready to feast and relax.

But John Smith would have none of it. "We're no savages, living from day to day! We must be ready to shelter the new settlers when they come!" He rationed the food supply; he drove the men relentlessly.

The men grumbled and muttered. The ships would have plenty of food, wouldn't they? And they would be here any day.

"We don't know when they will be here!" The captain hammered the words home. "We don't know! We cannot see across three thousand miles of ocean and know what has happened! So we must be ready for anything! To shelter them if they come—to survive without them if they don't come!"

"But we think—"

"I'll do the thinking and you'll obey orders!"

All day the axes rang, the saws snarled, and the hammers

beat their patterned tattoo: *thunk* . . . *thunk* . . . and three sharp raps.

As David worked, he fumed. If the London Council wanted to appoint a governor for life, why didn't they appoint John Smith? Who had done more? Finally what he was thinking boiled over in words to the captain.

"Englishmen are used to obeying a title," the captain said. "When Spain sent the Invincible Armada against us, Lord Howard was appointed head of our fleet—but Drake was the brains."

"I still don't see . . ." David muttered.

"Then your head hasn't grown as fast as your legs!"

The captain grinned and David finally grinned, too. In the two and a half years since he had left England, his legs certainly had grown! He towered over John Smith; he could stand eye-to-eye with almost any man in Jamestown. Now he looked down at John Smith and remembered some of the things he had planned to do when he was big enough. What a child he had been!

August came. No sign of Sir Thomas Gates and his nine ships. The men of Jamestown stopped grumbling and began to worry. What had happened?

"We don't know," John Smith said again. "That's why we must be ready for anything."

Mid-August, four battered ships crawled up the James, sails in shreds, some half de-masted, men toiling at the pumps to keep two of them afloat. When their passengers came ashore, some cheered, but others were sobbing.

David saw old Tim on the *Blessing* and hurried aboard. As he reached the deck, he heard a familiar voice aft, and wheeled. Captain Archer stood on the poop with the master of the ship.

"I doubt if John Smith is still alive," Archer was saying. "By now, the men of Jamestown will have risen against him. He's the biggest rascal unhung in the new world."

David leaped to the poop and confronted Gabriel Archer. "For your information, sir, John Smith *is* alive! In fact, since last February he has been the only survivor on the council. When you see what we've done, you may change your song!" Without waiting for an answer, he leaped to the main deck and went forward.

Tim chuckled and slapped him on the shoulder. "More like your father every day, lad! He'd be proud of you!"

David grinned, then sobered. "Too bad Archer's back. He's a troublemaker."

"And not the only one," Tim said. "Martin's on the *Falcon.* Ratcliffe's commanding the *Diamond*—if she weathered the hurricane."

David looked about the deck and up at the rigging. "I can see you've been through a storm."

"I didn't say *storm.* I said *hurricane.*"

"Worse than the storm we ran into just off Virginia in 1607?"

"That?" Old Tim spat. "Compared to a hurricane, that storm was just a rock-a-bye." He looked over at the other ships. "Four of us so far. Five still missing. We know one ketch went down. Lost with all hands. We saw her sink, and couldn't do a thing to help."

A bit later they joined Red, on the *Falcon.*

"How's the captain?" Red asked.

David told him what they had been through, and of how they had worked in spite of it. "Even the gentlemen worked."

Red's little eyes gleamed. "Good for the captain! When the men on the *Falcon* see what he's done, they won't pay so much attention to what Martin says against him!"

"Martin's talking against him, too?"

Red grinned and thwacked David's shoulder. "Don't worry, lad. Wait till the *Sea Venture* gets here with Sir Thomas Gates! Any bickering starts, and he'll lay them by the heels! Yes, sir! Things'll be all right soon!"

"Maybe," Tim said. "But if the *Sea Venture* went down . . . all the leaders on her . . . Gates, Admiral Somers, Captain Newport . . ."

Red jeered. "That's old Tim! Never a cheerful word!" He winked at David.

For once David could not smile with Red. If the *Sea Venture* had gone down, what would happen? John Smith's year as president would be over soon. Then what?

A few days later another ship limped into port—the *Diamond*, under Captain Ratcliffe. She was more battered than the first four had been—one mast gone, another sprung, and two feet of water in the hold. When they moored her at James Island, the passengers came ashore slowly, dazed, as though they still could not believe they had been saved.

Two more of the nine ships reached Jamestown, but not the *Sea Venture*.

"The thing to do," Captain Archer said, "is to set up a

council and take command until Lord Delaware gets here."

The gentlemen of the third supply shouted agreement. A council! That was the thing! They certainly weren't going to live under a tyrant like John Smith! *He who does not work cannot eat!* Hah! They had come over here to help rule the colony—not to sweat as common laborers!

Once more Jamestown was full of factions. Day by day the frown lines grew deeper between John Smith's eyes, and his voice had more of a bite.

One evening he sent for David and George Percy.

"Now what?" Master Percy muttered as they entered the cabin.

The captain was crisp. "Master Percy, I'm going up-river to bargain with the little Powhatan for his village. Remember it? What an excellent site? On the high bluff? He's willing to sell—cleared land, houses, gardens, palisades."

"A new town?" Master Percy asked.

"Before Lord Delaware comes, we'll need more room. We'll settle one group up the James; then we'll finish the new fort. After that, I'll bargain for another site, down-river."

"You . . ." Master Percy hesitated. "You are going to be gone from Jamestown quite a bit of the time?"

The captain nodded. "I'm leaving you in charge. Keep the work moving. If you have any idlers, lay them by the heels."

"I don't know . . ." Master Percy said. "These new men—they seem to feel they are under the command of

Sir Thomas Gates. I don't quite know what we can do to—"

"Build more stocks! And every idler can take his ease in them! With his wrists and ankles fast between two logs! I'm counting on you!"

Master Percy sighed. "Yes, Captain. I'll take charge. But—when the third supply goes back to England, I'm going along. I've had enough of Jamestown."

"I know." John Smith gripped his shoulder. "If we can keep control till Gates and Somers get here . . ."

"You still hope for that?"

The captain's smile flashed. "Hope for the best and be prepared for the worst! That's my rule!" He stood. "David, I want the *Discovery* and the shallop readied for the trip upriver."

"Aye, aye, sir!" David was glad he was going upriver with the captain. He would not have wanted George Percy's job!

Soon, with Francis West and a group of men, John Smith sailed up the James and bought the site for the new town.

Francis West scowled down from the high bluff. "But why should we settle up here? It'll take us a week to lighter a ship when a supply comes!"

"We aren't going to depend on ships from England forever," John Smith said. "We're going to be self-supporting, with our own livestock, our gardens, our fields!"

"But if—"

"You'll settle on the land I've bought for you!"

Sullenly the men landed and toiled up the bluff with

their possessions. When the *Discovery* was lightered, the captain ordered her to return immediately to Jamestown. He watched with a grim smile as the sails disappeared downriver.

He looked about the palisade of the town he had bought. "The Indians build well," he said. "They choose their sites well, too. We couldn't have a more healthful spot!"

The men shot lowering glances at each other and did not answer. The captain sighed and gave command to the men who were to return with him in the shallop.

On board he said, "You can pilot her, David?"

"Aye, aye, sir!"

The wind was brisk—very brisk—but fair.

"Waken me if it comes a blow!" The captain stretched out and closed his eyes. After a time, he slept. His face was haggard; he frowned in his sleep and muttered. Troubled, David looked at him. A year ago last Christmas, with the threat of death hanging over him in Powhatan's village, the captain had slept like a child.

If only Sir Thomas Gates is there when we get back! David thought. He did not look toward the captain again, for the wind had freshened. A man needed all his wits about him to pilot the boat down the treacherous river. The tide turned and was with them. David grinned. It took a bit of handling, but they'd never made such good time with the shallop before!

A sudden gust threatened to overset them. They struggled to get the shallop under control. Should he waken John Smith? The sleeping man was so miserably tired . . .

But I had my orders, David told himself, and if I don't

obey . . . As he turned, an explosion echoed and a sheet of flame enveloped the captain. Before the crew could make a move, John Smith plunged over the side.

"Keep your eye on him!" David yelled to one man, as they fought to bring the boat around. The minutes seemed endless before they could fight their way back upstream, for wind, tide, and current all forced them downstream.

When they got him aboard, David saw the charred patch from the captain's doublet down onto his trousers. His powder pouch had exploded. Carefully, David began to pick away the charred cloth. The last layer brought skin with it, exposing a circle of raw flesh a foot across. David gulped and fought nausea for one sick minute.

"Captain! Captain Smith!" One of the men spoke urgently. "Captain! . . . Unconscious. Let's pray God he stays that way till the . . . till we get back to the fort."

David looked at him quickly. That was not what the man had meant to say. The fellow did not believe they'd get the captain back to Jamestown alive. David wondered himself. Almost a hundred miles down the river . . . and not a thing they could do to help him.

CHAPTER EIGHTEEN

A Man to Depend on

BACK in Jamestown, the doctor took one look at the wound, and swore all the time he was covering it with ointment. David was alone by the captain's bed when George Percy came in.

"Captain? Captain Smith?" John Smith opened his eyes. "I've talked to the doctor," George Percy said. "He insists that the only thing for you is to go back to England."

John Smith nodded. He frowned, as though trying to collect his wits. "Gates?"

"Not yet."

Again the captain studied. "Delaware?"

"No." George Percy smiled ruefully. "I'll give you my

berth for the voyage to England. I guess my place is here until Delaware comes."

"Good man . . ." He looked at David.

"Yes, sir. I'm staying!"

David left George Percy with the captain, and went to see what he could do to help the sailors. It would take all hands to repair the hurricane's damage. They were leaving the small ketch *Virginia* at James Island. The six other ships would go back to England with word of the latest disaster—the loss of the *Sea Venture*. No hope now that she had not been lost with all their leaders.

David was working on the *Blessing* when a man joined him. It was James Gray of the *Phoenix*—who had been so sure his friends would "put some spirit in Jamestown."

"Warren, Captain Archer is the man to talk to if you want to go back to England, isn't he?"

"I don't know. And I don't care. I'm staying."

"You are? I thought—"

David grinned at him. "I belong to the original company —that 'sorry lot.' I came here to help plant a colony, and I'm going to do it!"

James Gray flushed. "All right! But I think I'll talk to Archer!"

Five minutes later David heard him shout, "No! I've nothing to say! *No!*"

That evening James Gray joined David and the doctor when they came out of John Smith's cabin. "Do you know what that infernal Archer is doing? Writing up charges against John Smith! He has a list as long as your arm! The men going back to England are fellows who will tes-

tify against him! Anyone who has a grievance can go—
and if you don't have a grievance, Archer will help you
think of one!"

"And you?" David asked.

James Gray bit the words out. "John Smith is, without
any doubt, the toughest, meanest man I ever knew! Just
the man, I'd say, for the toughest, meanest job an English-
man ever faced. You're staying, Warren?"

"I am!"

"Then I'm with you!" He shook hands, wheeled, and
strode away.

David looked at the doctor. "Why, those—those—"

"Don't worry," the doctor said. "When Lord Delaware
arrives in Jamestown, John Smith won't need any defenders. His work will speak for him."

"But in England?"

The doctor's eyes were sad. "He won't live to face his
accusers, David. If he lives till the ships sail, he'll be
buried at sea."

Stunned, David returned to the captain's hut and took
over the watch from Amos Todkill.

"What is it, David?" Amos asked.

"The doctor . . ."

"I know, lad. You hadn't been hoping, had you?"

For days the captain lay, eyes closed, seldom stirring.

Time and again, David thought the end had come.
But after a motionless pause, the captain would gasp
another shallow breath.

The night before the ships were to sail, David sat by the
captain's bed.

Toward morning John Smith stirred. "How is it with Jamestown?"

"Just fine!" David declared.

"Delaware?"

"Not yet. But he'll be here soon. Any day now."

"Too late for me. I'd like to be here when . . ." The words drifted off with a sigh.

David's heart hammered. Was the captain talking of the voyage to England? Or did he know the end was near?

"David?"

"Yes, sir?"

"I'm glad you're a man to depend on. I've orders for you."

"Yes, sir!"

"Forget me. Keep your tongue between your teeth."

After a while David said, "I'll keep my tongue between my teeth, sir. I promise you that."

The captain's mouth quirked. Then pain drenched his face with sweat. Presently he stirred and spoke again, more slowly.

"We called it a free land, didn't we? It was not free. It was dear-bought. But we have paid the price. I'd like to be here when Lord Delaware comes. I'd like to tell him . . ." He sighed and slept.

At dawn the doctor came to examine his patient. At last he shrugged, and nodded for the sailors to carry him aboard. David watched until the last sail disappeared down the James. That night he sat alone in a cabin he shared with four other men—all newcomers from the third supply.

Amos Todkill came with two other soldiers. They brought a candle and a paper. "Davy," Amos said, "we've a favor to ask of you. We've written a piece about him, and we'd like neat copies for—well—for quite a few of us."

"It's quite a bit of writing," one said, in gruff apology. "But you can take all the time you need."

"I'll make all the copies you want," David promised. When they had gone he grinned as he started to read the piece that was "quite a bit of writing."

. . . Thus we lost him that in all our proceedings made justice his first guide, ever hating baseness, sloth, pride and indignity more than any danger; that never allowed more for himself than his soldiers with him; that upon no danger would send them where he would not lead them himself; that would never see us want that he had, or by any means could get us; that would rather want than borrow, or starve than not pay; that loved action more than words, and hated falsehood and covetousness worse than death; whose adventures were our lives and whose loss our death.

David blew out the candle and bowed his head on his folded arms. Tomorrow he would make their neat copies. But not now.

Captain Ratcliffe called from outside the door. "Warren! David Warren!" David did not answer.

"Perhaps it's his watch," a strange voice said.

"We'll see him tomorrow," Ratcliffe answered. "You won't have any trouble striking up a friendship with him. You come from the same sort of background."

"You can depend on me."

"Good. Only we'll want you to be mighty subtle about

it." Ratcliffe's voice faded now. "We want him on our side. He's going to be one of the leaders of Jamestown. So when you start undermining John Smith . . ."

After a while David knelt by the fireplace and lighted the candle again. Dry-eyed, he began to make copies of the paragraph that was "quite a bit of writing."

The next morning Captain Ratcliffe brought a tall, handsome young man to meet David. The captain was jovial. "David Warren, have you met Roger Sanders? I've wondered if he could bunk with you? So many of the settlers are older . . ."

"Certainly. There's room for one more in the cabin. Only . . ." He smiled down at Ratcliffe. "If he tried to undermine John Smith, he'd have to be awfully subtle. Come along, Roger, and I'll help you get settled."

In the cabin, Roger shot a sidelong glance at David, started to speak, stopped, and finally laughed. "Aw, let's forget the whole silly business. Ratcliffe is a prince of a man, but that was a fool idea!"

"I think so. Besides—I had my orders: forget John Smith. That's what he ordered before he sailed. 'Forget me. And keep your tongue between your teeth.' "

Roger blinked. "Well, I'll be . . . You know, all I've heard of him—well, I thought he was the sort of man that I'd . . ."

"Want to bash over the head now and then?" David grinned. "Exactly. I remember once, when I cooled off, I found I had a rock in my hand."

"But in the long run?"

"I was just an undersized younker when I came,"

David said. "I used to ache to be big enough to face up to him. Now, I just hope to . . . measure up."

"We're going to get along!" Roger said.

"Right! The thing now is Jamestown."

They shook hands on it.

Master Percy sent for David. "I've organized a council, David, to take charge of things until Lord Delaware gets here. It seems the best way to get co-operation. . . ."

"Ratcliffe, Martin, and Archer?" David asked.

"Yes. After all, they are experienced. I'd like you for recorder. Only . . ."

"I know. I promised the captain I'd 'keep my tongue between my teeth.' After all, as the doctor said, when Lord Delaware gets here, John Smith won't need defenders; his work will speak for him."

George Percy nodded, then his eyes clouded. "October now. Delaware was to sail in August. I hope he gets here soon. Of course, we're well supplied." He shook off his mood. "Then you'll be our recorder?"

"With my tongue between my teeth," David said.

He had to keep reminding himself of that promise, when the council met.

"Now that John Smith is gone," Captain Ratcliffe said, "we won't have any trouble with the Indians. I think they really want peace."

President Percy nodded slowly. "I remember our last trip to Powhatan's village. He begged us to lay down our arms—to come as brothers."

Ratcliffe's smile was one-sided. "But of course John Smith would not do it?"

"No."

David felt his ears get hot. Had George Percy forgotten the warning of the Warraskoracks? That Powhatan had sent for them to put them to death? That he would lull them with fair words and cut their throats? Had he forgotten how Pocahontas came to them, heartbroken, to warn them against her own people?

"Yes," Ratcliffe said again, "with John Smith out of the way, we'll have no trouble with the Indians."

"And we've plenty of food," Archer said. "Delaware should be here any day. Certainly before the end of October."

But October ended; November came and passed. No sign of Delaware. Daniel Tucker, their cape merchant, asked to talk to the council.

Mr. Tucker was worried. "Our stores are running low."

"They couldn't be!" Martin said. "All the food we had!"

"But gentlemen, five hundred men have been feasting on those stores. And they *have* been feasting."

"Just how short are we?" George Percy asked.

"On short rations, we can last three months. Until the end of February."

"That's nonsense!" Captain Ratcliffe said. "The thing to do is to trade for a good supply of corn. I'll go. I'll take the pinnace and the ketch, both. I'll bring back enough corn to last till next harvest if we need it!"

With fifty-odd men the *Discovery* and the *Virginia* sailed. All the men were from the third supply. Captain

Ratcliffe was not going to have any men, he said, infected with John Smith's attitude toward the Indians.

Roger sailed with Captain Ratcliffe. "Look for us back before Christmas. David! We'll be plowing along, scuppers under with corn!"

They were not back before Christmas, but the council did not worry. After all, it was quite a trip to Powhatan's village. They might have been snowbound on the way. They'd be back soon. In spite of Mr. Tucker's worried face, the council ordered up a feast for Christmas. They had known enough grim Christmases—the first, windbound in the Thames—the second, when they thought both Newport and John Smith were lost—the third, when they were snowbound on their way to Powhatan's village. This year, they would not sit around and shiver. They would celebrate Christmas!

The year ended; 1610 began. The *Discovery* and the *Virginia* were not yet back with corn. Mid-January the council sent David and a dozen men in the shallop to Hog Island to butcher meat. It was then they caught sight of the pinnace and the ketch—toiling up the James, not "scuppers under with corn," but riding high in the water.

David took one look toward the ships, and was glad he had the shallop filled with men. "We'll forget Hog Island!" he said. He ordered the shallop alongside the *Discovery*, sent half his crew aboard her, and then went with the others to the *Virginia*.

"Make fast the shallop and tow her," he ordered. "They need us on board."

They boarded the *Virginia*. Roger was there, hollow-

eyed, dazed. Sixteen men—the survivors of Ratcliffe's expedition—were trying to bring the two ships back to James Island.

"Powhatan was so—so—merry," Roger whispered. "So friendly! He called us *brothers!* He said, 'Lay down your guns! Come as friends, and I will load your boats with corn.' Captain Ratcliffe believed him. Our men put out their matches; they laid down their guns." He looked at David, shaking his head. "I tell you, he was so friendly! Captain Ratcliffe sent some of us back to the ships to bring the copper. Then we heard the yelling . . . We . . ." He stopped and shuddered.

After a time, he went on. "I tried to reach him. I jumped overboard. I got ashore. But our men were surrounded by Indians. I couldn't reach him, but I was close enough to see." His eyes were dark with horror. "They had tied Captain Ratcliffe to a tree. They had built a fire in front of him. They scraped the flesh off his bones—gouged it off —and threw it in the fire—while he was still alive! They —they—" He could not go on.

Almost as dazed as Roger, David sat by him, wordless. Captain Ratcliffe and three dozen men tortured and killed; the Indians drunk with power. What would happen now?

When the council heard the report, they sat in shocked silence, too.

At last George Percy spoke. "We must have corn. Perhaps one of the tribes up the James . . ."

But survivors of the settlement upriver reached Jamestown with grim news; the Indians had risen against them, too.

"We'd better forget about trading," Archer said. "Delaware will be here any day; why should we risk our lives? All we have to do is to hang on a few days—a few weeks."

George Percy's frown was troubled. "But what if it is longer than a few weeks?"

"How could it be? He was collecting money and men for the expedition when we left England! He'll be here any day!"

David could "keep his tongue between his teeth" no longer. "How do you know he'll be here any day? What if he's becalmed? We were! We expected to be here in six weeks, and it took us four months! What if—"

"Bah!" Archer jumped to his feet. "Why doesn't someone cram his mouth and stop his talk! Just because John Smith is not here, he thinks no one else can manage Jamestown! But we can! Ratcliffe's expedition—that's very regrettable—but there's no sense in losing our heads! The thing to do now is to keep cool and wait for Lord Delaware!"

"We'll need to take stock of supplies," George Percy said, and sent for Mr. Tucker. "If we are rationed," he asked, "we have food for three months?"

"No, sir."

"But you said—"

"That was the first of December, sir. We haven't been rationing ourselves. Now, even with severe rationing, our food won't last two weeks. But we must go on short rations!"

"That's nonsense!" Archer declared. "Delaware will be

here any day! What's the point in starving ourselves, making our men sick?"

They killed the livestock that was left. By the end of January, there was nothing. They scrabbled about for roots; they tried to fish, but the fish were not running.

Mid-February, Indians came with baskets of corn on their backs. *Food!* The starving men cheered.

The spokesman for the Indians knew a bit of English. Did they want food? The Indians were ready to trade food for guns.

Some of the men protested, but others shouted them down. Why keep their guns? They could not eat guns, could they? When Delaware came, they would have plenty of guns! They fell over each other to be first to bring guns.

"We have much corn," the Indian spokesman said. "We shall trade as kings. Bring all the guns you can spare, and we shall give you much corn."

They stacked guns outside the fort. Higher and higher. The Indians scowled and muttered together. Was that all the guns they could spare?

By now the men were angry. "Yes! That's all!"

The Indians seized the guns; they set down half the baskets of corn they carried, and started off with the rest.

"Come back! Come back! More guns! More guns!" the men pleaded. But it was no use to yell. The Indians had gone. The men fell on the baskets of food, and fought over them as a pack of wolves. Some ate too much, and were sick.

The food lasted three days.

Indians came again to trade—more arrogantly than before; more and more weapons were stacked outside the gate; they gave less corn.

After March, the Indians came no more. The starving men still hoped. When Delaware came . . . Then one day David noticed something with a shiver. They no longer talked of Delaware. They had stopped hoping.

CHAPTER NINETEEN

Surrender

MARCH and April passed. It was May. David sat up slowly and looked about the hut that he and Roger had shared with four others. The two of them were alone in it now. The other four had died. He looked toward Roger's bunk and saw that it was empty. I hope he is all right, David thought. Roger had been talking strangely the last few days. About the lucky dead. The living were the unlucky ones—the living who wakened each morning to feel hunger gnawing, who lived in a half-world, too weak to know, to think, or to work, too hungry to sleep.

Roger came to the door, walking slowly, shuffling his feet, hanging on to the doorway for support.

"How many today?" David asked.

"Ten." Roger slumped on his bed. "Nine dead yesterday. Eleven the day before. Just ninety-two living now. Ninety-two men out of five hundred. In a week it will all be over."

"Unless something happens to save us."

Roger didn't bother to answer in words. His eyes said it for him; nothing could save them now.

"Pocahontas used to come," David said. "She used to bring us food. I remember once a tall warrior came with her, carrying a deer over his shoulder. We roasted the deer—"

"Stop it!"

"I'm sorry. But if Pocahontas came—"

"She won't." Roger slumped forward, his elbows on his knees, his scarecrow hands dangling. "She has never come since *he* went back to England." His eyes stared at nothing. An eerie flatness crept into his voice. "Pocahontas won't come . . . Pocahontas won't come . . ."

David's scalp crawled. That was the way some of them had sounded when they went mad. "Roger!"

Roger was silent; he shook his head slowly, from side to side—just a little motion, scarcely more than a tremble.

"Roger!"

The head-shaking stopped. "Yes, David. . . ." He wiped his hands down over his face, as though he had walked through a cobweb. "I wonder, if I sneaked into the woods—"

"No! You'd never get back alive! Remember what happened to Kent? He wasn't out of sight of the fort when the Indians killed him!"

Roger's mouth twisted. "What's wrong with that?"

David tried to clench his fists, but his fingers only curved, like claws. "We can't give up!"

"Why?"

"We've got to hold on until help comes!"

"When?"

"If we give up Jamestown, we've lost America!"

"Does it matter?"

"We've got to believe help will come!"

"It didn't come in time to save Roanoke."

"It did! If the colony had held on just two weeks longer, they'd have been saved! Just two weeks longer!"

"Help didn't come in time to save the second colony. They were deserted for three years."

"They were not deserted! It was because of the war with Spain!"

"Maybe there is a war now. How do we know? How do we know what is happening three thosuand miles away?"

A cold knot twisted in David's stomach, but he said, "Lord Delaware was to follow the other ships."

"Maybe he did. Maybe he followed the *Sea Venture*, right to the bottom of the ocean." His eyes began to stare again; the eerie drone crept back into his voice. "Lord Delaware and all his ships on the bottom of the ocean. Back in England, they don't know. They think we are a thriving colony. Men, women, children. Horses, pigs, chickens. Gardens. Back home, they are waiting for word from Delaware. Not worrying yet. Just waiting. Some day, they will began to wonder if something is wrong.

They will send another ship out to check on us. After a year or two or three. Some day . . . some day . . ."

David clawed at the wall and pulled himself to his feet. He stood a moment until his head stopped spinning. "Roger! Come on! They need our help!"

Roger wiped his hands down over his face again. "Yes, David."

Outside, David picked up their shovel. Only three shovels left in Jamestown. Three shovels for ninety-two men. But three shovels were enough. No one could dig very long. Some could not dig at all. Some never left their huts. They lay and stared at the wall and waited for the end.

While they worked, Roger seemed better. But that night he talked again in an eerie drone. "Some day, a ship will come. Too late. Just as the ship came to Roanoke. Some day a ship will come up the river, and anchor off James Island. They will hail us, and listen for an answer. Maybe they will sing English songs to let us know the ship is friendly. They will listen again. No answer. They will come ashore and look around a bit. They will sail down the James again. They will go home and report another lost colony. We'll never know, will we? We'll never know . . . We'll never . . ."

At last the drone stopped and Roger slept.

The next day seventeen died. Roger did not talk. When they had buried the dead, he sat by the gate that opened on the river, staring at the tawny water.

Toward sunset, he leaped up, shouting, "A sail! A sail!" He plunged into the river, swimming out through the empty water.

David lurched to his feet, but a voice stopped him. "Let him go. You couldn't save him. No use two dying for one."

It was true. Helpless, David watched. Roger swam straight out for a few strokes. The ebb tide caught him and began to bear him downriver. There was no struggle, no outcry, no flailing arms. He disappeared.

The next day fifteen died. Only sixty men left in Jamestown now; sixty men of the five hundred who had been there in October.

It was dark when the chore of burying them was done. David shuffled back to his cabin and felt his way to his bunk. He floundered to his knees. "Merciful Father, our strength and our defense . . ." He could not seem to remember more. He lay on his bed and repeated it. "Merciful Father, our strength and our defense . . ."

At dawn, a scream awakened him.

Another man had gone mad. Another man would be plunging into the empty water, swimming out toward nothing, disappearing. David pulled himself to his feet, shuffled to the open door, stared toward the river, and saw the sails of two ships.

Half the skeleton men of Jamestown were staggering or crawling toward the gate, screaming, "Food! Give us food!"

As David watched, the sails blurred and ran together; he felt the rough boards of the cabin wall scrape his back as he slid to the ground.

When he wakened, he lay on his bunk, dreaming that he smelled food. He shivered. Awake . . . and still dreaming he smelled food. That was dangerous. When men did that . . . He opened his eyes to banish the dream.

A tall young man bent over him, with a steaming bowl in his hands. David cried out and clutched at it.

The young man stepped back. "Steady. I'll feed you. Only a little at first, or you'll lose it." He spooned the broth into David's mouth. After a few spoonfuls, he stopped. "That's all for now."

David shut his eyes, fighting tears. The young man understood. When he spoke again, he had walked away. "My name is Rolfe," he said. "John Rolfe."

David open his eyes. John Rolfe stood in the doorway, with his back to the room. "More! Give me more!"

John Rolfe did not turn. "I was on the *Sea Venture*," he said. "We were wrecked in the Bermudas. Lucky thing, the way we were wrecked—that is, if we had to be wrecked. We were grounded, lodged between rocks. We had a chance to strip the *Sea Venture* before the waves beat her to pieces."

He came back to the bunk, and held out the bowl to David. "Here."

David tipped the bowl, drinking the rest of the broth. Some ran down his chin. He wiped it with his hand, and licked his hand. When he could trust his voice, he said, "How did you get here?"

"We built two ships. It took us ten months to do it. We named them the *Patience* and the *Deliverance*. A good name—the *Patience*."

"And *Deliverance* is a good name! You got here in time to save Jamestown."

John Rolfe did not answer.

"I prayed something would happen. And it did. You came in time! We'll make out all right now, won't we? . . . Won't we?"

After a while Rolfe said, "I don't know what we'll do. That is up to Sir Thomas Gates and Admiral Somers."

"They won't give up! We won't let Jamestown die, will we?"

Rolfe only said, "Think you can handle some more food now? We don't have anything very delicate. Just salted fish and salted pork. There were droves of wild hogs on the island. We had a dog with us. He killed the hogs. A good thing. We didn't have to waste our ammunition getting food. A bad business, when your guns are useless."

"Yes," David muttered, "a bad business." A bad business to surrender your guns, too. A bad business to trade your muskets for corn. It was good to have leaders who understood. Good to have leaders in Jamestown. He asked again, "They won't give up now, will they?"

"Lie quiet, now," Rolfe said. "I'm going to bring you something else to eat."

When he returned, Captain Newport was with him. At first, he said nothing. He only gripped David's hand. Finally he spoke. "Sixty men alive of five hundred. George Percy is right; we called it a paradise at first. It has been a misery, a ruin, a death, a hell. A slaughterhouse of Englishmen!"

"But we've hung on!" David said. "We'll not give up now?"

Captain Newport looked away. "I don't know, David. Our first job is to get you skeletons back on your feet."

For a week, the men from Bermuda cared for the survivors of Jamestown; they fed them; they washed them. At night, some of the men stayed ashore, but most of them went back to the ships. There were no cabins to shelter them.

David's strength returned so quickly that it surprised him. Even Captain Newport came out of his grim preoccupation long enough to smile. "You look as though you had gained ten pounds."

"I'm all right," David said. "When we start rebuilding Jamestown, I'll swing an ax with the best of you!"

Newport sighed. "It's no use, David. We don't have enough food. Just the pork and fish we salted. We knew we had plenty to get to Virginia. We thought, when we landed . . . And then we found this."

"But if we—"

"No. We checked our stores today. At the rate we're using them, we don't have enough for three weeks."

"If we could get corn from the Indians . . ."

"The way Ratcliffe did?"

David could not answer that. "If we could plant gardens . . ."

"Plant what? And live on what until harvest?"

"But we can't give up now!"

Newport frowned. "David, have some sense! More than four hundred men have died here in six months! Men who were well provisioned! What makes you think we could survive?"

"But when Lord Delaware comes—"

"There is no hope of that. His ships are lost."

"Not all of them! A storm might take one or two, but—"

"You've never seen a real storm, David. A hurricane could wipe out the navies of the world."

"You think Delaware—"

"Was lost months ago."

"Then . . ."

"We're having a meeting this afternoon."

David went to the meeting with lagging steps, knowing what he would hear.

Sir Thomas Gates spoke first. "The London Company sent me out to take charge of Jamestown until Lord Delaware arrived. I feel I owe it to England, and to the men who have died here, to see that we do not fail."

David could feel his heart pounding.

"But," Sir Thomas went on, "there is no chance of survival. We cannot even reach England with the supplies we have now. Our only hope . . . Admiral Somers, will you explain?"

"We shall weigh anchor as soon as the *Discovery* and the *Virginia* are seaworthy," Admiral Somers said. "We shall sail north, to the fishing banks off Newfoundland. If we find enough English fishing boats there, they can save us—take part of our passengers—supply us with food for the journey home. With luck, we'll reach England without losing any more men."

Captain Martin pulled himself to his feet, and spoke in a husky whisper. "Is there no chance, sir, to save Jamestown?"

Odd, Davis thought, the way men changed. Three years ago, Captain Martin had been too frail to stand the rigors of Jamestown. He had gone home for a year. Now, so weak he could scarcely stand, he was the one who wanted to hang on.

Most of the survivors muttered angrily. "No! Stay if you want to! We're going! Going before the rest of us die!"

Admiral Somers lifted his chin abruptly, and the gesture commanded silence. "Captain Martin, do you see any chance to survive? Any chance at all?"

John Martin stood, his lips tightening, the muscles working in his jaw. At last he sat down.

Admiral Somers said, "We'll need the help of every man who can help. The sooner we are at sea, the better chance we shall have."

The scarecrows of Jamestown cheered hoarsely.

David went back to his cabin, and knelt by his bed. He tried to pray, but no words came.

Jamestown had failed.

CHAPTER TWENTY

This Dear-Bought Land

DAVID sighed, got up, and went out to help with the work of readying the ships for the voyage. The *Discovery* and the *Virginia* were in bad shape; the holds half filled with stinking water; warped decks; frayed cordage. . . .

Maybe, David thought, they can't make these seaworthy. Maybe they will have to leave part of us here. Maybe they will . . .

But the men from Bermuda, who had built two ships, knew what they were doing. The night came when Admiral Somers said, "We sail in the morning with the tide."

Morning came; the drums beat a funereal roll; the men marched aboard. They cast off. The sails filled. One after another, the ships stirred and moved out into the James.

On board the *Patience*, David stood at the larboard rail, looking back on the palisade of Jamestown, remembering his last night at home—how his father and Uncle Rupert had talked of the first colony of Roanoke:

Father pounding his fist in his hand. "If we had held on just two weeks longer!"

Uncle Rupert taunting. "Yes, a pity you lost heart and gave up."

Father roaring. "I did not give up! No Warren ever gives up! If I had had my say, we would have stayed!"

Had Father felt this way, when they abandoned Roanoke? When Drake rescued them and took them home to England? Had he stood, straining his eyes for a last look at the land they had surrendered?

David grasped the ratlines, climbed, and clung, staring back at the fort. Just a spot now, lost between the wide, tawny river and the endless green of the forest. Lost . . . abandoned.

Tonight, the Indians would know. Tonight, they would celebrate. They would build great fires and dance a dance of triumph. Soon, the Spanish would know. They would lift their cups to toast the English failure. They would laugh because Spain had not had to send a single ship against the English. They had not had to banish them from the new world. The English had banished themselves.

The palisade faded from sight and was lost. Jamestown . . . David moved his chin against the ache in his throat.

That night he lay on the deck, staring up at the stars. A whippoorwill cried. An owl's hoot shivered and faded.

The spicy scent of pines came from the land. The free land, they had called it. It had not been free. They had paid a bitter price for it; three years of slaving work, of numbing cold, of smothering heat. Three years of sickness, starvation, and death. Three years . . .

He wakened and stared bewildered through the white mist that shrouded the world. Where was he? He felt the motion of the ship, and remembered.

The sun rose, and the mist turned gold. From high on the mainmast came the lookout's singsong, "Sail ho-o-o-o-o!"

David jumped to his feet, started toward the rail, stumbled over a sleeper, and sprawled.

"All hands on deck!"

Men lunged from the fo'c'sle, from the hatchways, stumbling over the sleepers.

"Cast loose your guns!"

A man bumped into David, and gave him a shove that sent him sprawling again. "Out of the way! It's the Spanish!"

"Take out your tompions!"

Battle orders! Spanish ships were in the James, blocking their way to the sea. David reached the rail, swung himself up, and leaned out to stare down the river, but the mist still hid everything.

From the quarter-deck, Admiral Somers hailed the lookout. "What colors does she fly?"

The lookout could not see colors yet; only the sail.

"Run out your guns!"

And, simultaneously with the orders to the gunners,

242

came the order to the crews to get the ships under way.

"Prime!"

The Spanish . . . with their huge, high-pooped ships, crowded with soldiers. No hope, David thought, but we will die fighting. He looked at his hands, and saw they were steady. I'm not afraid! Maybe it's because it is better to die fighting than to go home and confess a failure.

The lookout yelled again, then came scuttling down the mast. "The English! The English! A longboat, flying Lord Delaware's colors!"

Through the wild cheering, the measured commands:

"Put in your tompions!"

"The English! The English! Lord Delaware!"

"House your guns!"

"Lord Delaware! Hurrah!"

"Secure your guns!"

A captain came aboard from the longboat with the news; Lord Delaware's fleet was in the Chesapeake, with supplies for four hundred men.

David slid back to the deck before he fell, and slumped there, limp with the long exhaustion, but grinning. Maybe, he thought, by the time we get back to Jamestown, maybe I can stand up again. Maybe . . .

"You there! Bear a hand!"

"Aye, aye, sir!" Dazed, he found himself on his feet, saluting briskly.

"You can handle sail. Lay aloft!"

"Aye, aye, sir!" He cheered with the others as he climbed.

Back in Jamestown, he cheered with the others as Lord Delaware came ashore with a flourish of trumpets and a velvet-clad guard of honor.

But when Lord Delaware knelt to give silent thanks, David searched his mind for a prayer of thanksgiving and could not find the words; all he could remember was a prayer for the dying. He stared at the crimson velvet, the shining trumpets, but they could not banish the pictures of three years of dying:

Scurvy . . . one body after another, wound in its sheet, sliding into the sea.

Swamp fever . . . John Smith's bleak eyes when he stood by Gosnold's grave.

Starvation . . . men crawling, begging to trade their guns for food.

The Indians . . . George Casson dashing from the forest, falling, his arms outflung, the arrow in his back.

The explosion . . . John Smith, with death etched on his face, waiting to be carried aboard a ship bound for England, whispering, "It wasn't a free land. It was dearbought. But we have paid the price. I'd like to be here when Lord Delaware comes. I'd like to tell him . . ."

Lord Delaware rose from his knees and looked long at the ruins of Jamestown. At last he spoke. He had food, he said—for men who would work with a will to rebuild Jamestown. He had weapons, he said—either to defend them from their enemies, or to punish their wrongdoing.

"I hope I shall never lift a gun against a man of Jamestown. But," and his face was stern, "I shall do what I must do to save the colony. And my power is absolute; Governor General of Virginia for life!"

That night there was food from home: butter and cheese —roast beef put down in vinegar—mutton put down in butter—raisins and sweets. And there were letters from home. A man called David's name and passed a letter back to him.

David glanced at the letter:

David Warren
Gentleman of Jamestown

in an impatient scrawl. *John Smith!*

He ripped it open and began to read, torn between wanting to linger on one sentence and to race on to the next. John Smith had survived his burns; he was well again, and full of plans.

. . . I have seen six maps of our northern lands, all as different as night and day. No more use to me than scrap paper, though they cost me more. Soon I shall go to explore, and bring back a map men can depend on.

David smiled. When he had finished the letter he turned back to read part of it again:

We English have failed many times, but England shall not fail. Some day history will forget the men who failed and remember only our successes. History has a way of doing that. That is why ancient nations seem so wise and our own so foolish.

But all Romans were not Scipios; all Carthaginians were not Hannibals; all Genoans were not Columbuses.

We English are learning, slowly and painfully, that we must serve a long apprenticeship to become masters of colonization. We allow an apprentice seven years to master the skill of a simple trade. Why should we think half seven years can train us to be master colonizers?

But we shall not fail. We shall not forget Raleigh: "The wings of a man's life are plumed with the feathers of death." We shall not forget Gilbert: "Fear not. Heaven is as near by sea as by land." We shall not forget your father. "A Warren never gives up. A Warren never surrenders."

Men like those will keep the dream alive in England. Men like you will keep England alive in America.

Wherever fate casts my lot, I shall work for it, and fight for it. It is my life. It has been my hawk, my hounds, my wife, my child, the whole of my content—this dear-bought land.